THE ISLAND COUNTRY

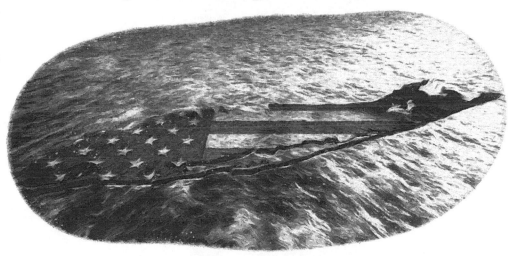

A NOVEL BY
RICHARD DAUB

Richard Daub

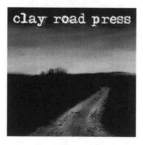

www.richarddaub.com

@rdaub82

It was cold and had just started to rain. On the front lawn, Detective Philip Smith of the Nassau County Police Department, wearing the formal Navy uniform he'd worn during the War, directed his family's attention through the leafless trees, to the top of the bank building several blocks away, on top of which an American flag waved against the gray sky.

He saluted, and his family did the same, his wife Eunice and three children, seven-year-old Philip Jr., five-year-old Joyce, and three-year-old Oscar.

"On this day, December seven, thirteen years ago," he began, "our great country was attacked in cowardly fashion by the Empire of Japan, killing over two thousand American servicemen and causing extensive damage to our Pacific Fleet. To all Americans who lost their lives that day, we will never forget."

From his breast pocket he removed his Hohner harmonica and played "Taps." It started raining harder. After the harmonica fell silent, the detective said, "Inside, let's go!" The children ran through the downpour towards the house, followed by their father.

Inside, removing his wet shoes, Oscar looked out the door window at his mother still on the lawn saluting.

"Daddy, why is Mommy still outside in the rain?"

Detective Smith looked outside, then back at his son. "She's okay, pal. She'll come inside in a minute."

"Daddy, why did the Japanese attack us?" Joyce asked.

"Because some people are evil."

"Then why do Japanese people live in America?"

"That's a damn good question. We let them in, then they attack us. We had to build internment camps and lock them up during the War because we couldn't trust them. I still don't."

Mrs. Bernadette Fisch, kindergarten teacher and former starving artist who'd once had some of her paintings displayed at an art gallery in the Berkshires, going around the classroom looking at her students' crayon drawings, stopped at Table D, where she'd placed the do-nothings and troublemakers, and where sat Joyce and her partner-in-crime, Dolly, with the fiery red hair, who was absent today.

"Oh," uttered Mrs. Fisch, leaning in for a closer look at the masterful shading, a bright red rose on a textured stem with ultrasharp, almost metallic-looking thorns surrounded by rich green leaves, the contrast of beauty and danger—

"Oh, Joyce, oh, dear—did you really draw this?"

The girl nodded.

"Joyce, this is magnificent! And all this time I had no idea you were such a talent! You should do more!"

Eunice Smith, "Burner of Roasts", five-foot-four and weighing under a hundred pounds, acorn hairdo, fast-talker, sometimes frozen in place and other times zipping around the house like the old Chaplin pictures, burst into the house and began going in and out of rooms, looking under beds, searching the basement, lifting couch cushions, until finally locating the rusted Maxwell House coffee can on the kitchen counter.

She removed the lid, revealing a rainbow of pills prescribed by Dr. Peterson to treat her "condition". She scooped a handful and dropped them on the counter, then separated them by color. The few violets and indigos she combined into a pile of purples. There were plenty of reds, oranges, yellows, greens, and a few blues.

She separated two of each color and moved them into a single pile, then scooped the excess from the counter and dropped them back into the can and replaced the lid.

She opened the refrigerator and removed the bottle of Tropicana orange juice and placed it on the counter.

"Eunice," said the girl on the label, Tropic-Ana, shaking her grass skirt, causing an orange to fall from the bowl atop her head, "drinking glasses are dangerous. You should drink straight from the bottle."

"Oh-kay!" Eunice said, then twisted off the lid. She scooped the pills from the formica and looked at them in her palm.

"You can do it, Eunice!" Tropic-Ana cheered, swinging her fist.

"Oh-kay!" Eunice said, then threw the pills into her mouth and gulped them down with the juice, some dribbling down her chin.

"Now put me back, please," Tropic-Ana said.

"Oh-kay!"

After putting the bottle back in the fridge, she picked up the Maxwell House can and brought it into the living room. She stuffed it between two couch cushions, looked around, pulled it out, brought it back into the kitchen, and placed it in the exact spot on the counter it had been. She then turned and headed out the front door.

She climbed into the Buick and, for the next three hours, sat motionless with both hands on the steering wheel.

She then burst into the house and began going in and out of rooms, looking under beds, searching the basement, and lifting couch cushions, until finally locating the rusted Maxwell House coffee can on the kitchen counter.

Philip had just taken a bite of his sardine sandwich when the doorbell rang.

"God damn it!" he said, mouth full, sardine juice streaming down chin. He dropped his cloth napkin on his plate and got up. "Who do these people think they are?"

Joyce and Philip Jr., the bespectacled aspiring pastor clad in homemade clerical collar, watched their father steam across the living room to the front door. Oscar, the aspiring fireman, wearing replica firefighter helmet given him during a visit to Santa at the fire station, looked for a moment, then took the first bite of his fourth peanut-butter-and-jelly sandwich.

In the kitchen, Eunice was frozen in place in front of the open refrigerator.

Philip pulled open the front door, leaving the storm door closed. On the stoop stood a black man and woman, in their sixties or older, well-dressed, the man wearing a dark, pinstriped suit with matching fedora, the woman a long black overcoat and leopard-skin pillbox hat.

Both were holding copies of *The New World Translation of the Holy Scriptures*, the Jehovah's Witness bible.

"Go back to your own neighborhood!" Philip ordered through the storm door glass. "I'm a police, and if you're not off my property in sixty seconds, I'm gonna run you in for trespassing!"

The man and woman helped each other down the steps. About halfway down the walk, the woman slipped on a patch of ice and nearly fell, but the man was able to catch her and hold her up.

Philip opened the storm door.

"Don't let me catch you in our neighborhood again!" he called.

"Class," said Mrs. Fisch, holding up Joyce's drawing of the rose for all to see, "I just wanted to share with you this wonderful artwork made by one of our very own students. This, believe it or not, was done by Joyce Smith, right over there at Table D. That's right, you heard correctly, *Table D*, where the naughty children sit. Class, why don't we all give Joyce a round of applause."

She started clapping, and the other children started clapping, except Dolly.

"You drew that?" Dolly asked Joyce.

"Yep."

Dolly laughed.

"What's so funny?"

"You're an artist!"

"What's so funny about that?"

"My daddy says art is for Tinker Bells."

"What do you mean?"

"You know, fairies. You're a fairy!"

"Am not!"

Officer O'FlannerO'hann rose when Detective Smith came in.

"Is it my wife again?" the detective asked the traffic cop.

"Yes, sir. She was stopped at a red light, foot on the brake. Bit of a traffic tie-up, but we straightened it out and drove her home and she seems okay now."

"Thanks, O'FlannerO'hann. And, as usual, let's keep this quiet, eh?"

"Yes, sir. I will, sir. I'm hoping to make detective someday too, sir."

"You're on your way, kid."

Joyce stood before her father, he wearing the frilly, flowery, yellow-and-white, stain-splotched baking apron he wore in his basement workshop while crafting his birdhouses, napkin holders, paper towel posts, toilet paper stands, and "wall art"—Nutcracker-inspired wooden soldiers, Snow White, the Seven Dwarfs, Cinderella, Goldilocks—a talent none outside the house were aware of, pieces Eunice would attempt to sell at the Trinity Lutheran seasonal craft fairs under strict orders to say she made them if anyone asked.

"So, whaddaya think, 'lil girlie?" he asked, holding his two latest pieces of wall art, Peter Pan and Tinker Bell.

"They're nice, Daddy," she said, then turned and ran to the staircase, bursting into tears on the way up and locking herself in her room.

"You seem a little off today, Mrs. Smith," said Dr. Morris Peterson, lighting a Lucky Strike and shaking out the match. "How are you feeling today?"

"I'm a cement truck," Eunice said, hands on an imaginary steering wheel, making truck noises.

"That's what I was afraid of, Mrs. Smith. But this is your lucky day, because I just received samples of a brand new kind of medication that the Army has been experimenting with on their soldiers. It's called—"

He picked up the pill bottle on his desk and put on his reading glasses—

"Lysergic acid diethylamide 25—try saying that five times fast. The boys at the club are just calling it LSD. Why don't you take this bottle here, and take one of these pills every morning when you wake up—just one, only one—and then just take the other pills per usual, as needed. Do you understand, Mrs. Smith?"

Eunice pulled an imaginary string above her head and made a truck horn noise.

Through the living room window, Joyce watched her father back the unmarked police cruiser out of the driveway, then pull away.

Her mother was giggling in front of the television set turning the vertical hold knob back and forth.

Ten minutes later, Philip Jr. left for school.

Oscar was still at the table eating the leftover donuts their father had brought home from the station and served for breakfast with glasses of milk.

Joyce went down to the basement and took the Tinker Bell wall art from her father's workbench and wrapped it in his yellow apron, then brought the bundle upstairs and stuffed it in her backpack.

Walking to school, she went down the alley behind the chop suey restaurant on Hempstead Turnpike, behind which was a dumpster with a lid too heavy to lift. She removed the bundle from the backpack and left it on top of the dumpster, then continued to school.

That afternoon, the bundle was gone.

"Eunice!" Philip called from the basement. "Do you know what happened to my Tinker Bell? And my apron?"

He waited for an answer, then went upstairs and found his wife in the dining room with crayons and sheets of loose leaf paper all over the table and floor, the papers covered with scribblings of the full Crayola color palette.

"Eunice, just what in the goddamn hell are you doing

now?"

She stopped scribbling and looked at her husband, smiling oddly, looking past him.

"The colors," she said.

"Yes, very nice, Eunice. Have you seen Tinker Bell and my apron?"

"There's Tinker Bell! She's flying around your head! And she's wearing your apron! Oh-kay!"

"Good God, Eunice, you're even more cuckoo than usual. I'm going to have to have a talk with Doc Peterson to get you some stronger pills."

The house was quiet, Joyce and Oscar not yet home from school, Father at work, Mother sitting out in the car.

Philip Jr. passed through the kitchen and dining room and back out to the living room. He listened at the bottom of the stairs that led up to their bedrooms, and at the top of the basement stairs, then went into his parents' first-floor bedroom.

Most of his mother's dresser drawers were partially open and all manner of apparel was hanging from them. He looked into the top drawer at the mess of loose socks and underwear—no bras, there being so little to support—then started digging, until he'd found four pairs of silky briefs, all yellowed with age and dappled with old stains.

He spread them foursquare atop the dresser and adjusted them until they were precisely aligned, then smoothed out the wrinkles.

He looked at himself in the mirror above the dresser, then left the room, returning moments later wearing the clerical collar he'd stolen from St. Thomas, the Catholic church, during their Christmas craft fair, and nothing else.

"Alright, little girlie, here she is, even better than the original!"

The new Tinker Bell wall art was even more vibrant and twinkling than the original, and larger, almost as big as Peter Pan. And there were more characters—Captain Hook, Wendy Darling, Little Ronnie, the Lost Boys, Tiger Lily, Smee, Slighty.

Her father's new lavender apron flared below the waistline.

"Well, girlie, whaddaya think?"

"It's nice," she said, looking away.

"Say, how about a little celebration? Whaddaya say we all go out for chop suey?"

The Smith family walked the three blocks to the restaurant, the night air fresh after the earlier rain, the wet streets sparkling under the streetlamps.

Philip was about to open the restaurant door when, in the window, hung beside the red neon "Best Great Chop Suey" sign, he noticed his original Tinker Bell wall art piece.

"What the hell is this? Eunice, do you know anything about this?"

His wife, giggling in front of the neon, tracing the letters on the glass with her finger, did not answer.

Philip looked at his daughter.

"Do you know anything about this, girlie?"

She shook her head and looked away. Her father looked at her for a long moment, then at his sons, before pulling open the door.

The restaurant was crowded and steamy and smelled like

rice and cigarettes. Most of the patrons were men wearing Navy uniforms, and there was a group in the corner wearing leather motorcycle jackets and caps.

"Ship must have come in," Philip said, looking around the room. Several sailors were looking at him. One winked. A mustached man in a leather vest puckered his lips.

"Mrs. Lee," he said to the hostess, "where did you get that Tinker Bell in the window?"

"We find on top of dumpster wrapped in apron. Apron dirty and we use as rag, but Tinker Bell nice, we put in window. Bring lots of business."

"I can see that," he said, looking around the room, then at his giggling wife waving a pair of chopsticks in front of her face.

In his younger sister's bedroom, Philip Jr. smoothed the wrinkles from the four pairs of briefs spread before him when, in the mirror, he glimpsed the large sketch pad sticking out of the closet.

"Holy Mother of God!" he exclaimed, holding the pad open to a pencil drawing of their father, nude, only his police cap atop his head and his service belt around his waist sagging under the weight of the loaded gun in the holster, detective badge in open palm, penis unflatteringly small and flaccid.

There were nudes of the entire family, and more sketchbooks and canvases in the closet, many unflattering of family members. The ones of herself were beautiful, the lost artist, sad, innocent. Dolly was a temptress, large, powerful, fearless.

After he was done with the underwear and had put it back in the drawer, he brought the artwork across the hall to his and Oscar's room, then waited at the front door for his brother to get home.

"We must burn these evil works," he said, showing them to his brother. "I need you to stand by as fireman in case the blaze gets out of control."

"They look like Joyce's."

"Yes, it seems our sister has been possessed by the devil, and this is the result."

On the back patio, Philip, in full clerical garb, and Oscar, in firefighter raincoat, helmet, and boots, looked at the small, seldom-used charcoal barbecue.

"It's too small," Oscar said. "You should use the garbage can."

At the end of the driveway, the brothers dumped the contents from one of the steel trash cans, then began filling it with Joyce's sketchbooks and canvases. He then pointed the can of Wizard Charcoal Lighter Fluid at the pile and squirted until it was empty.

Oscar stood ready with garden hose, hand on nozzle.

"Dear God," said Philip Jr. to the cloudless blue sky, "we stand before you today to destroy this filth created by the hand of our beloved sister through the evil spirit of Satan, who has sunk his talons into her innocent soul. We pray in Jesus' name, amen."

He struck the match and tossed it into the trash can. A tower of flame erupted, the heat knocking both backwards before the flame settled into a steady burn.

They turned when they heard the Buick door open behind them and watched their mother climb out. Leaving the car door open, she headed towards them saying, "Pretty fire."

"Stay back, Mother," warned Philip Jr. "Allow God to do his work."

Oscar stood pointed the nozzle at her, but she stopped ten feet from the can, smiling.

"Pretty fire," she said.

The fire was still burning when they heard the car door close and saw Joyce approaching in the driveway.

"What are you guys burning?" she asked. "I could smell it from two blocks away."

"For the love of Christ," said Detective Smith, behind the wheel of his unmarked police cruiser, turning onto Morton Avenue from Hempstead Turnpike, then pulling next to the curb in front of the Munson house, where the Jehovah's Witnesses were on the front walk heading back towards the sidewalk, white-haired Mrs. Munson at the front door watching.

Detective Smith got out of the car and waved to Mrs. Munson. She smiled and waved back. He then turned to the Jehovah's Witnesses.

"I thought I told you two to stay out of our neighborhood."

"This is a free country," the man said. "At least it's supposed to be, anyway."

"Horace, no," the woman said.

Detective Smith looked at the house.

"Mrs. Munson," he called. "Can you open the door a moment?"

Mrs. Munson opened the door enough to stick her head out.

"Mrs. Munson, did these people ring your doorbell and start harassing you with their Jehovah's Witness business?"

"Yes, Detective Smith, that's exactly what they did."

"Were you frightened, Mrs. Munson?"

"Oh, yes, Detective Smith," then, in a rising tone, "I was afraid for my life!"

"I'm sorry to hear that, Mrs. Smith. You can go back inside, I'll take it from here."

"Thank you, Detective Smith. It's men like you who make this country great."

He turned back to the man and woman.

"See my car there? Why don't you two go behind it and put your hands on the trunk. I'm sure you know the routine."

The detective read them their rights, patted them down, confiscated their Bibles and other belongings, handcuffed them, and put them in the back of the car.

Neighbors watched from front doors and living room windows, nodding, smiling, waving to their detective behind the wheel of the cruiser as it pulled away, the bowed heads of the man and woman in the back seat windows.

Eyes wide, red hair ablaze in the gray television glow, Elvis singing "Don't Be Cruel" on the other side of the glass, Dolly turned the volume knob on the Zenith all the way up, his golden voice drowning the shouts of her father in the next room whipping her mother with his belt as she cried at him to stop.

Then his shouts were in the room as he burst into the den and ripped the television cord from the wall socket.

Breathing hard, he pointed the belt wrapped around his

wrist at his daughter.

"I catch you watching that crap again and this goddamn box goes right in the trash can. Now, you stay right here, Red, you're next after I'm through with your mother."

Eunice, having just finished her session with Dr. Peterson at his New Hyde Park office, now behind the wheel of the Buick, turned out of the parking lot onto Jericho Turnpike heading east, then turned right onto 12th Avenue South, towards the grade railroad crossing.

Bells started ringing. Red lights started flashing. The gates started coming down. The slow-moving Buick cleared the first gate, but not the second, and stopped on the tracks.

"Pretty lights," Eunice smiled, foot on the brake, the blaring horn to her right getting louder at the approach of the eastbound express, sparks streaming from its wheels as the engineer pulled the emergency brake, but too late, the train still traveling over 50 MPH when it reached the crossing.

Roger Ramsey, alone in the house he shared with his older sister, Belinda, his legal guardian since their parents passed, pressed the cheerleader spankies to his face and, hand inside his briefs, inhaled deeply and held it as long as he could before exhaling.

Moments later, he did the same with another pair of spankies from the hunter green-and-white cheerleader uniforms he'd pilfered from the girls' locker room at Valley

Stream North High, where he sometimes attended with his best friend, Fred Flynt, who'd just let himself in the house and walked into Roger's bedroom as he was exhaling.

"Still sniffing those things?" asked Fred, voice gravelly from smoking Winstons since he was ten, one of which he lit now, his waistline expanding daily since being kicked off the football team for poor grades.

Roger tossed the spankies aside.

"Forget those things," Fred said. "We need pussy."

In the second floor girls room at West Hempstead High School, Joyce and Dolly were in front of mirrors fixing their Aqua-Netted hair with cigarettes burning between their fingers, Joyce with her Breck-blond bangs and pink lipstick, Dolly with her copper red bangs and aquamarine eye shadow, when the door flew open and two sophomore girls burst in—

"Ringo is cuter!"

"No! Paul is!"

The girls halted and fell silent upon noticing the seniors glaring at them.

"News flash, ladies," Dolly said, approaching the girls, flicking her cigarette at them, both jumping back to avoid being struck, "the Beatles are deviant homosexuals."

"Please don't hurt us," one of the girls said, both about to start crying.

"Then, *girls*, don't come bursting into *my* ladies' room gushing about those sissies. Let me give you a piece of advice—go home and listen to a real American man like Bobby Rydell."

"We love Bobby Rydell!" one of the girls said, both

nodding.

"Oh yeah? Name one of his songs."

They looked at each other.

"Wildwood Days?"

"Lucky guess," Dolly said, leaning in until both were in her shadow. "Now get out of my ladies room!"

"You want me to sign this garbage?" asked Fred Flynt Sr., at the kitchen table looking at his son's report card, reading glasses on, Lucky dangling from lips, empty tumbler and ashtray in front of him. "Four F's and a C? What the hell's the matter with you, Freddy? You tryin' to wind up a bum on the street corner?"

"I'll be alright, Pop."

"Alright? You're flunking. You know what happens to guys who flunk out of school? They get sent to Vietnam, and, if they're lucky, they come back in one piece. And if they don't have a diploma when they get home, they get jobs at the factory, or they turn into bums on the street corner. And that's exactly where you're headed."

"I've got a plan, Pop."

"What plan? Selling goddamn light bulbs?"

"That's right."

"That's it? You'll sell light bulbs. Just like that."

"That's right, Pop."

"Jesus Christ, Freddy. The way you're going, you'll never amount to anything but bein' a bum on the street corner. Alright, where's the goddamn pen?"

Joe the bartender placed a glass of Schlitz in front of Detective Smith and a glass of chardonnay in front of Detective Beasley.

"Philip," said Detective Beasley, putting a hand on Detective Smith's forearm, "I know it must be tough without Eunice, so, if you ever feel lonely or just need someone to talk to, you're always welcome at my pad. We can talk, or watch a Western, drink wine, sit around in our drawers—"

"Our drawers? Whaddaya mean by that, Bruce?"

"Well, I have a bachelor's pad, so there wouldn't be any women bothering us. We can sit around in our drawers, drink, smoke, wrestle, do whatever we want. We'd have complete freedom to be the men we are."

"You got a point there. I always thought it would be more comfortable just wearing my drawers around the house, but there's always someone around, and then there's always someone knocking on the door, like the goddamn Jehovah's Witnesses."

"They never bother me at my place."

"Oh yeah? That must be nice. Peace and quiet. I wish I had that at home when I'm down in the basement."

"The basement? What do you do down in the basement, Philip?"

"Handyman stuff, I guess. I have a little workshop down there. I work with wood. Make things."

"What kinds of things do you make, Philip?"

"Oh, this and that. Household items. Crafts."

"Crafts? I love crafts. Say, Philip, I could really use a handyman like you at my pad. You can even work in your drawers if you want, I wouldn't mind at all, believe you me. Maybe I'll even join you. We can drink some wine, look at some magazines, shuck some oysters—"

"Oh yeah? I haven't shucked oysters in a while."

"Philip, I'll handle everything. Just show up in your tool belt. And, I promise, no women or children. We'll be like Hemingway, men without women. It'll be fabulous. We can even do some police drills if you're in the mood."

"I do still enjoy police drills."

"Also, they're showing *Pal Joey* on the tube as the *Saturday Night Movie of the Week*."

"Fine picture."

"Terrific picture. You have Sinatra, and all those women in their beautiful outfits."

"It all sounds swell, Bruce."

"Wonderful, Philip. Why don't you come over Saturday afternoon. How does 2:30 sound?"

"We have to do something," Fred said, handing a can of Schlitz to Roger, seated in a lawn chair on the back patio.

"What should we do?" Roger asked, pulling off the tab and dropping it into a metal bucket filled with them.

"Start a gang."

"A gang? Like *The Little Rascals*?"

"No. Like Marlon Brando."

"Oh. Don't we need motorcycles for that?"

"Nah. We just need to look cool like them. And grow mustaches so we look older. That's what the girls want."

"What girls?"

"The girls who put out. The ones who like guys like Marlon Brando and James Dean. The girls on the corners."

"What corners?"

"The corners where the gangs hang out."

"Oh, yeah. Right."

"We just have to tag a vacant corner. I've been asking around. The corner down the street near Dan's is free."

"Who else is gonna be in the gang?"

"Maybe a few others."

"Oh."

"We also have to get some motorcycle jackets and patch them with our name and logo. I was thinking The Red Devils."

"The Red Devils?"

"What do you think?"

"Cool."

"Good. I'll take care of the jackets. We'll tag the corner tonight."

"We should look for boys in Franklin Square," Dolly said to Joyce.

"Franklin Square? Isn't that where all the gangs are?"

"I'm tired of West Hempstead boys. I think they're all homosexuals."

"Why?"

"Because we're the prettiest girls in school and none of them ever ask us on dates."

"I think they're just shy. Some boys are intimidated by pretty girls."

"Then I want a man who isn't intimidated and knows what he's doing and not some candy ass who pisses his pants playing back seat bingo. I want a man who's gonna make it all the way. I want a king, and I'll be his queen."

"And you think you're going to find this man on a street

corner in Franklin Square?"

"Maybe. There might even be one over there for you too."

In a cone of streetlight on the corner of Dogwood and Sprague in Franklin Square, across the street from the Dan's Supreme shopping center, long considered a loser corner by the other gangs in the hamlet, having been abandoned by the likes of The Fluffs, The Mailmen, The Barbers, The Florals, The Nickel Steaks, The Panzees, The Clams, The Oysters, The Joneses, The Mickeys, The Turks, The White Castles, and a dozen other fly-by-night outfits, stood Fred and Roger, mustaches grown—Roger's a biker-style handlebar extending down his chin, Fred's a pencil stache like Jackie Gleason—wearing leather jackets patched with the devil logo from the can of Red-Devil quick drying enamel that Fred had brought with him to the patch store and the fronts patched with their official gang names—Roger's being "The Ram", which a gym teacher had called him once while taking attendance, and Fred's "Slate", a reference to Fred Flintstone's boss—tight blue jeans rolled up at the cuffs above engineer boots, and, despite the late hour, ditty-bop shades, holding cans of Budweiser, cigarettes burning between fingers, The Ram smoking Viceroys, Slate smoking Winstons.

"Tonight's the night," Slate said.

"I hope so," said The Ram. "Being in a gang is getting boring. We've been standing here for three weeks and nothing's happened."

"Be patient, like a hunter in the weeds. The patient ones get the big game."

"We're almost out of beer. And I'm almost out of smokes.

And I have to pee again."

"I'm getting tired and my feet really hurt," Joyce said, "and so far all the Franklin Square guys have been total losers."

"Just a little further," Dolly said. "He's close. I can smell him."

"The king?"

"There," Dolly said, pointing towards a red glow hovering against the night sky, the neon sign atop the Dan's Supreme supermarket.

As they got closer they saw two silhouettes in the corner lamplight across from the shopping center, one tall and lean, the other tall and stout.

"There he is," Dolly said. "My king awaits. You can have the beanpole."

Behind the wheel of his Plymouth Fury, a retired police cruiser his father had helped him purchase, the police lettering and insignias still partially visible beneath the white paint job, Philip Jr. turned onto Ivy Street where, up the block, an older black man and woman were retreating to the sidewalk in front of the house belonging to the even older, broom-wielding, screaming Mrs. Morris—

"It couldn't be," said Philip Jr., pulling next to the curb.

The Jehovah's Witnesses stopped when they reached the sidewalk and watched the tall, slender young man in the clergy suit step out of the vehicle.

"Let's go, Horace," the woman said, taking him by the arm, but he didn't budge.

"He ain't no clergy," Horace said. "He ain't no cop either."

"Get out of our neighborhood!" Mrs. Morris yelled. "Scram!"

Philip Jr. stopped on the sidewalk several feet from them.

"My father told you to stay out of our neighborhood."

"Your neighborhood," Horace said, shaking his head. "This ain't your neighborhood, son. This is America."

"Now we can take the girls to the drive-in, or wherever we want," Fred said, showing Roger the cobalt blue 1962 four-door hardtop Chevy Impala he'd just purchased.

"Where'd you get the dough for this?"

"Selling light bulbs."

Inside the small, unventilated office shared by the West Hempstead High School freshman and junior varsity football coaching staffs, Coach Ziegerwold leaned back in his squeaky chair and looked Oscar in the eye.

"I'm sorry, son," he said. "You're just too fat to play ball. Now go clean out your locker and leave the helmet and pads with the equipment manager."

It was between the second and third of a triple-feature during their first double-date at the Green Acres Drive-In, featuring *In Like Flint*, *The Adventures of Bullwhip Griffin*, and *Casino Royale*, when Joyce and Roger, on line at the snack stand, shared their first kiss, a peck on the lips, then another on the way back to Fred's car, Roger holding Joyce's hand and the tub of popcorn they were going to share during the Bond film.

Both stopped short when they saw the Impala rocking wildly and heard Dolly's muffled yells, "Fred! Stop, Fred! No!"

"Maybe we should go back to the snack stand," Roger said.

Ignoring him, Joyce ran to the car and tried to open the rear passenger door, but it was locked. Through the window she saw Fred's bare ass and Dolly's hair below him on the back seat. She tried the other doors, but they were also locked. Back at the rear passenger door, she slapped the window with her palms and shouted, "Fred, stop! Leave her alone!", but he didn't stop until letting out a low, gravelly moan.

"Dolly!" she yelled. "Dolly!"

"I'm okay!" Dolly called from inside.

Fred pulled up his pants then, reaching behind him, opened the door and crawled backwards out of the car.

Out of breath, on the other side of the open door from Joyce, he finished zipping and buckling.

"Wished it was you, don't you?" he said to her. "I know I did."

Atop the rubble and ash of what had been the Kingdom Hall of Jehovah's Witnesses in Roosevelt, megaphone in armpit, lighting a Tiparillo, Detective Philip Smith faced the crowd of angry residents, all black except one white family with a girl and an awkwardly tall, curly-haired boy with a large nose.

"You did this, whitie!" someone yelled.

Through the megaphone he responded, "I'm here to find out who did this, and, when I do, I promise, I will bring them to justice. But right now this is a crime scene, so why don't you all scram and let us do our job."

Megaphone off, he turned to a uniformed officer.

"Harris, why don't we have this place taped off? Let's get some tape around here, wide perimeter, so we can keep these goddamn people the hell out of our way."

"Yes, sir."

"You know what tonight is, Delores," her father said, at the kitchen table, chewing steak.

She waited before responding.

"Yes."

"No sneaking out till I'm done with you."

No response.

"Answer me, Delores."

"Yes."

"Good. Now fix me another steak."

"So, little girlie," Philip started, having just swallowed a mouthful of sardine sandwich, "what exactly are you planning on doing after graduation?"

"I don't know. And I'm not your 'little girlie' anymore."

"What is your friend Delores gonna do?"

"Secretary school. But I'm not doing that."

"Then what are you gonna do?"

"I said I don't know!"

"You don't know?"

"I'll sell my paintings. Paint new ones. Sell those."

"Do you honestly think someone's gonna buy that filth of yours you call 'art'? Try making a living that way and you'll wind up selling your paintings on a street corner like Hitler."

In the kitchen, an hour before her father's alarm clock would ring, Dolly uncapped the bottle of Four Roses bourbon, then retrieved the can of Rat-Tox from under the sink and flipped open the cap. She squirted some into the bourbon, then re-capped the bottle, sloshed it around, and returned it to the liquor cabinet.

She squirted some into the orange juice and all over the coffee grounds in the can of Maxwell House Western Blend.

She sat at the table and emptied the pack of Chesterfields and added a single drop to each end of the nonfiltered cigarettes, then replaced them in the pack and cleaned up the loose tobacco strands.

She looked around the kitchen, then re-capped the Rat-

Tox and returned it under the sink exactly as it was.

Back in her room, she pretended to be asleep until the alarm clock rang.

"Shouldn't you have your nose in a book, boy?"

Fred Jr. stopped at the front door and turned to his father.

"I asked you a question, son."

"No. I'm going out."

"You're going out. Again. And not hitting the books."

"I don't need those books."

"Goddamnit, Freddy, when the hell are you gonna get your head out of your ass and wake up?"

"Don't worry about it, Pop."

"Don't worry about it? Don't worry about it? And just what in the hell is that supposed to mean?"

"It means I'm gonna make something of myself, and not wind up a miserable, broken-down failure like you."

"You think I'm a failure, Freddy? You think I'm a failure? Just lookout, kiddo. You're on your way to being something worse. A bum. That's all you'll ever be, Freddy. A goddamn bum on the street corner."

It was dusk when Dolly got home. Her father's car was in the driveway and the house was dark.

She opened the back kitchen door.

"Hello?" she called.

No answer. She turned on the light.

There were dishes from breakfast in the sink. Coffee cup, orange juice glass, plate with yellow egg smear and bacon bits. Pack of Chesterfields on the table, several butts in the ashtray.

She heard a noise in the bathroom.

"Daddy?"

She found him on the floor, on his side, in front of the toilet. There was vomit and blood in the bowl and on the floor.

He looked at her pleadingly and opened his mouth, but no sound came. He appeared unable to move.

"Oh, hi, Daddy," she said, cheerfully. "Hope you had a nice day. You know what tonight is. It's the night I'm going out and staying out really, really late, so don't wait up for me."

"Quite frankly, Roger, I'm a bit concerned for your welfare," said Mr. George Meisler, Guidance Counselor, Valley Stream North High. "Your grades... attendance... lack of aptitude... no plan to speak of... no chance of getting into college... I'm not even sure the community college would touch you at this point... Roger, are you with me?"

"Yes, sir."

"Roger, do you know what happens to boys with records like yours?"

"No, sir."

"They get sent to the jungle in Vietnam."

"Are there snakes?"

"Snakes?"

"Are there snakes in that jungle?"

"Oh, yes, lots of snakes. Biggest in the world, and the most poisonous species. But, listen, Roger, I've got a solution for you. The Army has a special early enlistment program for boys such as yourself, the ones good at staring off into space. If you sign a letter of intent right now, they won't send you to Vietnam, but to a nice, quiet country that has no snakes, or at least very few, where you'll spy on the Soviets. You see, Roger, they've been able to find plenty of boys to send over to Vietnam to get shot and have limbs blown off, and get bitten by snakes, but they've been having a difficult time finding men who can handle staring off at a blank horizon ten, twelve hours a day. Apparently, staring at nothing all day takes a special talent, and your teachers have told me that you, sir, have such a talent. Roger, the United States Army is looking for boys—men—just like you. They'll even throw in free cigarettes. Interested?"

Only one couple remained on the gym floor during the last dance at the Valley Stream North High School Senior Prom, the hunter green and white balloons beginning to deflate, the spiked punch gone and only spent fruit rinds left in the bowl, the band playing Bobby Rydell's "Swingin' School" after being given a generous tip.

"Let's go to Coney Island," Fred said to Dolly, the song coming to an end.

"I want this night to last forever," she said, kissing him.

"The night's only getting started. Come on."

It was a lovely June evening, crescent moon in a starry sky above the dim buzzing lights of the emptying parking lot.

"What's that smell?" Dolly asked.

Ahead of them, two hippies were leaning against Fred's Impala smoking a joint. Parked next to it, a Volkswagen Microbus loaded with more hippies, above it a large cloud of smoke wafting in the parking lot light, *Sgt. Pepper's* on the stereo.

"God they're disgusting," Dolly said. "So filthy. I can't stand them."

"Stay here," Fred said.

The two hippies leaning against his car stopped smoking and watched him approach.

"Hey, Fred," one of them said. "Want a hit? It's good shit. Hey, man, what the fuck—"

Fred grabbed him by his fringed, faux suede vest, lifted him off the asphalt, and threw him into the Microbus, prompting numerous screams and shouts from inside the vehicle. He did the same with the other one, then slid the door shut and leaned into the front passenger-side window.

"See my car right here?" he said to the mass of hair and beads in the back. "If you see it in the lot, park somewhere else."

"Sure thing, Fred," someone said.

The White Castle on Sunrise Highway in Lynbrook was crowded with couples who'd left various proms in the area, but Roger, in rented powder blue tuxedo, and, Joyce, in green gown torn slightly at the shoulder from the giant corsage he'd earlier pinned on her, had managed to secure a booth, and were now seated across from one another holding hands on the table, a tray of heavily onioned little hamburgers between them.

"Did you have fun?" Roger asked.

"Yes, Roger. I did. That's the fifth time you've asked me."

"Sorry. This has been the greatest night of my life."

"Yes, you said that earlier."

"Well, it has been."

"I believe you."

"And it's about to get better."

He reached into his coat pocket and pulled out a cardboard ring box with the logo for Ralph's Jeweler's at Green Acres Mall.

"Oh, God," she said.

Roger slid out of the booth and dropped to a knee.

"Oh, God," she said again, looking around, the restaurant hushed, customers and staff watching.

"Joyce," Roger said, removing the cover, revealing a ring with a modest, slightly misshapen diamond that the prongs were unable to keep secure as he pulled it from the box, the stone falling to the floor and bouncing around.

"Crap," Roger said, looking down. "Oh, there it is."

He tried to put the diamond back in the prongs, then gave up and put it on the table.

"Joyce," he said, looking up at her, the knee of his tuxedo pants soiled from kneeling on the greasy linoleum, "will you marry me?"

"Oh, Roger. Can I think about it?"

Halfway through the Tunnel of Love in Coney Island, the amusement car jerked to a stop.

"What's happening?" Dolly asked.

"Don't worry about it," Fred said.

"We're trapped!"

"We're not trapped. I paid the guy two bucks to stop the ride."

"You what? Why? It's dank in here!"

"So I could do this."

He reached into his coat pocket.

"Oh, Freddy, no, not in here—"

He pulled out a Tiffany ring box and opened it.

"Be my queen, Dolly."

"Oh, Freddy, yes, yes!" she exclaimed, voice echoing in the tunnel. "I'll be your queen!"

"I can't believe you're leaving," Joyce said to Roger, starting to cry. "I mean, I knew it was coming, but I was trying not to think about it."

They were on a Jones Beach lifeguard stand cuddled beneath a blanket, the endless black Atlantic before them under a hazy half-moon, having just finished a six-pack of Budweiser, the empty cans in the sand below, five on his side, one on hers, this their last night together before Roger would board a Greyhound bus in the parking lot of the Green Acres Mall to take him to boot camp in Fort Dix, New Jersey.

"Don't cry," Roger said, then began sobbing himself. "I don't want to go to boot camp! I'm scared they're gonna yell at me!"

Joyce held him tighter.

"It's okay," she said. "They're probably gonna yell at everyone, so try not to take it personally. And they said they were going to send you somewhere nice and quiet where there's no snakes or people shooting at you, so try not to worry too much. You'll be fine. Actually, I think I'd rather go with you than to beauty school."

"Then why are you going?"

"I don't know what else to do. I'm not good at anything except painting and doing my hair, and I'm not going to secretary school like Dolly. She's crazy. She's heard all the stories too, but she says she's not worried."

For several minutes they watched the breakers crash, then Joyce leaned over and kissed Roger on the cheek.

"I've made up my mind," she said.

Dolly knocked on the open office door of Larry Scott, Dean of the Brille Secretarial Academy, who was seated behind his desk.

"You wanted to see me, Dean Scott?" she asked.

"Yes, Delores, please come in, and shut the door behind you."

Dolly closed the door and sat in one of the two chairs facing his desk.

"Delores," he said, lighting a brown cigarette, "I have to be frank. You're a big girl, you're typing stinks, and you're rude. But you can still do well in this business—if you know what to do."

"Oh, my, Dean Scott," she said, batting her lashes. "I had no idea I was doing so poorly. What do I need to do?"

Dean Larry Scott rose from his chair. He was not wearing pants, and his erection was poking through the bottom of his dress shirt.

"Oh, Dean Scott," Dolly giggled, fingertips over mouth. "You're making me blush."

"No need to blush, Delores, and don't be shy. The shy girls don't last long in this business."

"Well, Dean, it's just that I've never seen one that *big*

before. I mean, you oughta be careful with one that big, you can injure a girl."

The dean looked at his erection begin to deflate, then sat back down.

"Okay, Delores, rule number one, don't ridicule your boss."

"But, Dean—Larry—can I call you Larry-cakes? I wasn't ridiculing you, it's just so *big*—"

"You're still doing it."

"No, really, Larry-cakes. Have you ever thought about acting in pornography films?"

"Alright, that's enough—"

"How are you even able to zip your pants?"

"Okay, Delores, you need to leave—"

"Can I see it again?"

"Please leave, Delores."

She finally rose and looked down at him trying to cover himself behind his desk.

"Your wife's a lucky lady," she smirked. "Her husband's got a small dick, *and* he cheats on her."

"Get out!"

"I've got some advice *for you*, Dean Larry-cakes. Make sure you can handle a woman before you show her that pathetic little thing."

"Out! Out! Out!"

In her Lynbrook apartment, Becky Barker was in the bathroom finishing her makeup when the doorbell rang.

"Just a minute!" she called.

At the door was her beauty school partner, Joyce.

"Hey, sexy," she said. "Ready for your practice perm?"

"Yep. Ready for yours?"

"For sure!"

The kitchen table was covered with permanent wave rods, towels, combs, capes, clips, scissors, and bottles. On the counter there was a bottle of red wine and a pack of Parliament cigarettes with two marijuana joints on top of it.

Becky uncorked the bottle and poured two glasses, then began setting Joyce's hair in the rods. After they were in place, she squirted them with the bottle filled with water, then set the kitchen timer clock.

"Have you ever tried pot?" Becky asked.

"Pot? Oh, God no, my father's a cop."

"Bummer. Would you like to try some? I have a couple of joints right here."

"I don't know. It won't make me psycho, will it?"

"Not at all. It'll relax you and give you a new perspective. Artists use it all the time."

She showed Joyce how to inhale from the joint and told her to hold it in her lungs as long as possible before exhaling.

Joyce took two hits, then lit a cigarette as Becky started rolling her hair.

"Feel anything yet?" Becky asked.

"Just the wine."

Becky was reaching for another rod when her breast brushed against Joyce's cheek.

"Sorry," Becky said.

"It's okay," Joyce said.

Becky smiled. Joyce Smiled back. Becky leaned in to kiss her, but Joyce pulled away.

"What the hell are you doing?"

"I thought you said it was okay."

"I said it was okay when I thought it was an accident!"

"It *was* an accident!"

"Was trying to kiss me an accident too?"

"No, but you said it was okay."

"It's not okay! I'm Christian!"

Joyce got up and tore off the hair cape.

"I'll take these out myself at home," she said, then grabbed her purse and stormed out of the apartment.

Rhonda emerged from the bedroom.

"I take it my fantasy of a threesome this evening is a wash," she said.

"I had no idea she was such a square," Becky said. "This whole time I thought she knew and was just being cool about it, but, after tonight, I'm thinking she's just some totally naïve God-loving fool or something. I mean, Jeez Louise, everyone else at school knows. And she'd never even smoked grass before! It's like she just climbed out of a time machine from 1956!"

Visibility inside the International Arrivals terminal at Istanbul's Yeşilköy Airport was low, only the odd beam of late afternoon sunlight able to penetrate the gaps in the thick fog of tobacco smoke as hurried travelers who couldn't see more than three feet ahead routinely collided and burned each other with their cigarettes, including Roger, with chevron mustache, carrying an olive-green hardshell Samsonite suitcase, wearing a flowery red Hawaiian shirt, a pair of Levi's with khaki web belt, white sneakers without socks, aviator sunglasses, and a Detroit Tigers home cap.

For nearly an hour he'd been unknowingly walking in an

oval when he bumped into a man dressed just like him, except his Hawaiian shirt was blue and he was wearing a Los Angeles Dodgers cap.

"Hello, fellow American tourist," he said. He too had a chevron mustache, and, though he couldn't have been more than a couple of years older than Roger, his teeth were yellow and tarred at the gums and one of the bottom ones were missing. "Can you tell me where I can find a nice hotel at a reasonable rate?"

"The Howard Johnsons is my hotel of choice," Roger said.

"Good. Follow me. There's a car waiting outside if we can find our way out of here."

"Can you imagine?" Dolly bellowed at Joyce across the diner booth table covered with the remains of their breakfast, ashing her Virginia Slim on a plate smeared with eggs and syrup. "Three days camping on a farm surrounded by filthy, drugged-out hippies? Ugh, it makes me sick just thinking about it!"

"Yeah," Joyce laughed, ashing her Kent on a plate of unfinished French toast.

"Who would go to that much trouble when Bobby Rydell and Elvis aren't even on the bill?"

"Sha Na Na's gonna be there."

"Yeah, but I'd rather see them at the bandshell than with a bunch of filthy hippies running around with dirty bare feet peeing in bushes and copulating in public. And there won't be any bathing or showers!"

"Sounds gross," Joyce said, sipping her coffee, looking out the window at the traffic on Sunrise Highway.

Becky poured two glasses of red wine and brought them to the living room.

"I don't know, Rhonda," she said, handing her one of the glasses and taking a seat next to her on the couch. "I mean, you've seen her, she's a total square. I'm surprised she still even speaks to me after that night she came over when we were in beauty school. It's kind of weird. She still calls me sometimes to talk about music. I think she's lonely."

"My thinking, Becks, is that the little Swiss Miss Girl would be the perfect driver, while the rest of us are getting high in the back of the van. Her father's a cop, right?"

"Yeah."

"So, if we get pulled over, she can probably even talk us out of it."

"She did mention that she wanted to go, but has no one to go with. I felt kind of bad. And she's probably good for some gas money."

"We don't have to hang with her. Once we get there, it's gonna be everybody for themselves anyway, and we can find her when it's over. Maybe there'll even be some other squares she can hang with and pray or something."

"Alright, I'll ask her."

At the Ahu Akbaba Resort in İğneada, on the Black Sea in the Kırklareli province, surrounded by the lush Yıldız Mountains, six miles south of the Bulgarian border, Roger had just tapped the first keg of the evening when the belly dancers arrived snapping their zils, prompting a round of cheers from the men.

"Ah, I see they sent the good ones tonight," said Sergeant Zale, cigar in hand, wearing a flowery green and yellow Hawaiian shirt and Oakland A's cap, waiting for Roger to pour his beer. "So, whaddaya think so far, Ramsey?"

"I like working the keg better than the watch shifts."

"I know what you mean. That's why we like to blow off a little steam in the evening after a long day."

"Are the other belly dancers coming?"

"Not, tonight, Ramsey, but I did put in your special request. There's a shop in Istanbul, Joe Camel's Western Wear, that we put in an order with for some football cheerleader uniforms, but there was some confusion over the 'football' thing, because when you say 'football' here, they think of 'soccer'. And they also have a different idea of what 'cheerleaders' are. Very different. You should have seen the looks on their faces when I mentioned the spankies. But don't you worry, son, I think we finally got it straightened out."

Most of the village had been scorched by the air raid and the surrounding jungle was still smoldering, yet, somehow, several huts had survived.

Bringing up the rear, Sergeant Flynt stopped at one of them while the rest of the platoon continued through the village and back out to the jungle.

He looked inside and met the eyes of a woman breastfeeding an infant, then entered.

"Put the baby in the crib," he ordered her in Vietnamese,

pointing to the baby, then to the crib.

The woman didn't move.

He repeated the command, louder, but still she didn't move. He removed his handgun from the holster and pointed it at her, then at the crib, then back at her.

She unlatched the baby and put it in the crib, then stood next to it.

"Take your clothes off," he ordered, but she didn't move.

He put the gun back in the holster and approached her. He threw her to the dirt floor and tore the clothing from her body, then stood over as he unbuckled his belt.

On the shoulder of Route 17 West between Rock Hill and Monticello, Merle Austin flicked his Marlboro to the gravel while his fellow roadies from Sweetwater, the band scheduled to open the festival, looked at the line of abandoned cars as far as the eye could see, and the tens of thousands of smoking golden people walking between them and on the shoulders and median on their way back to the garden.

"I ain't walkin'," Merle said.

"They're sending a helicopter," said one of the others.

"For the band. Not us."

"They'll figure something out."

Merle looked at the road, then back at his colleagues.

"Fuck this. I ain't following those tie-dyed lemmings. I'm outta here."

"Where ya going?"

"Back to the city."

"How ya gonna get there?"

"I'll figure something out."

The Econoline started knocking and jerking near Doodletown, just west of the Bear Mountain Bridge.

"Shit," Becky said, emerging from behind the mandala tapestry separating the driver and front passenger seats from the back of the van, bringing some of the pot smoke into the cockpit with her.

"What should I do?" asked Joyce, behind the wheel.

"Pull into that little parking lot up ahead."

They were inside Bear Mountain State Park at one of the recreation areas. Joyce pulled into a spot and cut the engine.

"It's the transmission," Becky said. "I can do a bush fix to keep her patched up to Bethel, but it's gonna take a couple of hours."

"I like bush fixes," someone said in the back, prompting giggles from the other girls.

There were two coolers, one packed with ham and American cheese sandwiches and cans of Coca-Cola, the other with bottles of off-label red wine. Joyce sat at a picnic table with the red-eyed girls from the back of the van, most of them eating voraciously, while a couple giggled at some ants on the table and one gazed deep into the forest.

After finishing her sandwich, Joyce went back to the van and retrieved her knapsack packed with blanket, pajamas, Colgate toothpaste, Kent cigarettes, sketchbook, and drawing pencils.

Becky and Rhonda were in front of the van, Becky's hands and forearms smeared with grease, her head beneath the open hood.

"I'm going for a little walk," Joyce said, knapsack over her shoulder.

"Okay, but be careful," Rhonda said. "There's a lot of psychos in these parks."

The Phoenician yellow '65 Mustang coupe convertible was just sitting there with the top down and key in the ignition, parked with the thousands of other vehicles on Route 17 West as the hippies streamed by, eyes fixed on the promised land.

Merle hopped in and sat behind the wheel. He checked the glove box and it was registered to someone in Scarsdale. He lit a Marlboro and watched the people go by, oblivious to his presence.

After he finished his smoke he looked around again, then started the car. He inched it backwards and maneuvered it out of the tight space, then through the stream of humanity and across the median to the vacant eastbound lanes.

Just beyond the recreation area, seated on one of the logs used to mark the end of the parking spaces, Joyce was sketching the Hudson River Valley before her when the yellow Mustang convertible pulled into the lot and parked at the other end.

The driver was wearing a white cowboy hat and v-neck t-shirt and had a sandy-blond handlebar mustache. He lit a cigarette and kept glancing at her as he smoked and she became too distracted to continue sketching.

When he was done with the cigarette he flicked it away and started the car. He backed out of the space and sat there a moment, then drove in reverse to her and stopped.

"Headed to *Woodstock*?" he asked.

"We were, but our van broke down."

"Where is it? Maybe I can help."

"It's back at the recreation area over there. My friend is fixing it."

"Well, I wouldn't bother going any further. The traffic's so bad up there that people are ditching their cars on the road and walking the rest of the way. Route 17's a damn parking lot."

"Were you going to the concert?"

"Yeah, I'm a roadie with Sweetwater—well, I *was* a roadie with Sweetwater. We were supposed to open this hippie-fest, but we got stuck in traffic and everybody started getting out of their cars. At this point the only way to get there is by helicopter or to park your car at the end of the traffic jam and start walking."

"That's crazy."

"Yep. That's when I'd had enough. You sure you don't need help with your van?"

"No, my friend said she could fix it, but I should probably go back over there and tell them about the traffic."

"I can give you a lift over there if you want."

"I don't know."

"What don't you know?"

"If I should get in a car with a stranger."

"You sound like my daddy. He's a cop and he always told me to never get into a car with a stranger."

"My father's a cop too."

"Oh yeah? Where ya from?"

"Long Island."

"Sure, we've done some gigs out there. I'm from Texas,

just outside Austin. That's my name too, Merle Austin. What's yours?"

"Joyce Smith."

"Pleasure to meet you Joyce. See? We ain't strangers no more, and our daddies are cops. I'm actually headed down to the city if you want a lift. If you'd like, I can swing back so you can tell your friends."

She looked back at the recreation area.

"Let's just go," she said.

"Let's just go," Rhonda said to Becky.

They were in the Econoline cockpit, Rhonda in the passenger seat with her dirty bare feet up on the dashboard, Becky behind the wheel, the rest of the girls in the back.

"What if she got kidnapped by some psycho who has her locked up in his cabin and is using her as his sex slave?"

"Well, there's sure as hell not anything we can do about that, and it's her own fault for wandering off by herself, so let's just go before the traffic gets bad. I don't want to miss Sweetwater."

"Fine."

Becky started the van and shifted into reverse. She pulled out of the space, then tried to shift into drive, but the gear selector wouldn't budge. She started shaking it until it broke off in her hand, then there was a metal-grinding noise, followed by a heavy thud.

"Shit," Becky said, tossing the remains of the selector onto the dashboard and cutting the engine.

"What was that?"

"The transmission."

"Can you fix it?"
"Not this time."

"I've never seen the city so empty," Merle said, pulling the Mustang next to the curb on West 23rd Street. "Look at all this street parking! I guess everyone went upstate, except Joni Mitchell."

He got out of the car and hurried around the front of it to open the door for Joyce.

"Thanks," she said. "Oh, you left the key in the ignition."

"That's alright. This is my friend's car. He told me to leave it like that."

"Isn't he worried someone's going to steal it?"

"Guess not. Say, I know you're headed up to Penn Station, but I'm stayin' at the Chelsea tonight, friend of mine has a room there I can use while he's up at the hippie-fest. Ever been? It's where all the weirdo musicians and artists live. I can give you a tour if you'd like, I've stayed there a bunch of times. Dylan used to live there, and that famous artist— Kooning?"

"Willem de Kooning?"

"That's him. William Kooning."

In the woods next to the recreation area parking lot on the west side of the Bear Mountain Bridge, Cephus and Mayter, cans of Genesee Cream Ale in hand, halted just before the end of the tree line.

"See that van over there in that there parking lot?"

"Yup."

"That ain't just any old van."

"It ain't?"

"Nope."

"Then what is it?"

"That right there is a van full of girls."

"Shoot. How do you know?"

"I seen them girls before. Van's broken down. They's all inside sleeping."

"Dad gum!"

"That's right. After we finish these Screamers, we should go pay them girls a wakeup call."

An earlier rain had puddled the neon-lit streets of Saigon's Scag Alley, now alive with mopeds, motorbikes, U.S. servicemen, prostitutes, and Fred Flynt, in the new suit he'd earlier in the day had custom tailored for pennies on the dollar—brown with white pinstripes, fedora with white band, mustard yellow shirt, tangerine tie, mustard socks, brown shoes freshly shined.

He turned off the main drag into a narrow alley and entered a three-story cinder block building with dozens of wires hanging from an awkwardly leaning pole on the roof. Inside was humid and smelled of rice and cigarettes. At the top of the third floor stairs he was greeted by an old man with a Kent in his lips who nodded and knocked on the metal door behind him. Someone inside pushed it open and the old man stepped aside and Fred went in.

On the factory floor, Mr. Pham, in white short-sleeve dress

shirt and brown slacks, was speaking loudly to the foreman over the noise of the machines, which were being operated by women and children.

"Ah, Welcome, Mr. Flynt," he said, extending his hand.

"Mr. Pham," Fred said, shaking has hand. "This place is a lot bigger than it looks from the street."

"We combine third floors of five buildings into one factory. We make bulb of every kind—for house, office, school, street, stage, flashlight, car, psychedelic—all for penny on American dollar. Less than penny. Fraction of penny."

"And you've got the shipping sorted out?"

"Yes. In cargo container. People inside container guard inventory. Make shipment to States every month on secret ship. Also penny on dollar."

"I like what I'm hearing, Mr. Pham."

"Yes, Mr. Flynt. We make good business partnership."

"I don't know what to do!" cried Joyce to Dolly, who opened her arms and led her to the couch.

"Sit down, sweetie, have a cigarette. I'll get some wine and then we'll talk."

Dolly went into the kitchen and returned with two glasses of red.

"It should have been a week ago," Joyce said. "Nothing. And I feel weird. But I can't go to Dr. Quincy because my father would find out, and, if I am, he'll kill me, and then he'll probably try to find Merle through his cop father."

"I've been there, sweetie. More than once. But there's a doctor in Chinatown who helped me, his name is Doctor Wu. He'll test you and, if you are, he does the procedure right in his office, and then it's over. And he helps with other stuff too that the regular doctors don't do. He even does plastic surgery and has his own line of ancient Chinese remedies."

"Chinatown? Is it safe?"

"It's safer than going to a doctor around here and having your father find out. His motto is, *When you don't know what to do, come see Doctor Wu.* I told him he should hire a jingle artist."

"I don't know if I could do something like that."

"And this cowboy has a wife and kid?"

"I think he has more than one wife. When I was in the bathroom at the hotel, I heard him call three different women. That's when I got dressed and snuck out. Who knows? Maybe there's more. For all I know, he could have been sitting there all day calling them after I left."

"So, unless you want to become another member of his harem and take care of his child by yourself—he's a roadie for some hippie band?"

"Sweetwater."

"Sweetwater? What the hell kind of name is that?"

"I don't know."

"So, unless you want to take care of his child by yourself with no financial support, and also lose Roger, and disgrace your family, I don't see what other choice you have."

"Oh God," Joyce sobbed.

"There, there, sweetie. Let it out now. Then we'll go see Doctor Wu."

In Bruce's living room, he and Philip, wearing ribbed tank top undershirts, Fruit of the Loom briefs, and black socks, sorted through the pieces of stained wood, nuts, bolts, screws, and other hardware and tools scattered on the floor.

"Philip, I can't even imagine what this is," Bruce said. "You stained this wood yourself?"

"Yep, down in the workshop."

"I'm impressed. I'm guessing it's a furniture piece of some kind."

"Fully functional furniture, you might call it. How would you like to be my apprentice while we put this thing together?"

"I'd love it, Philip—I mean, *master*."

The men worked throughout the afternoon to the blaring horns and swooning strings of the *South Pacific* soundtrack on the hi-fi. Philip did most of the hands-on work, while instructing his apprentice to *hold this* or *screw that* or *go mix us another couple of pink ladies*.

"I'm just dying to know what this is," Bruce said.

"I'm surprised you haven't figured it out already," Philip said, continuing to work.

When it was finished, it took up most of the empty space in the living room.

"I still don't know what it is."

"You don't know what this is, Bruce? It's a pillory. Like they had in the old days for public humiliation."

"Oh. Now I get it. I've just never actually seen one in person. How does it work?"

"Well, one fella puts his arms in the holes like so, and his head in the big hole, and then the other fella closes the top and locks it, and then people just come over and humiliate him. Here, let's give it a try. I'll be the prisoner, and you put me in it and humiliate me."

Bruce gently closed the top of the pillory over Philip and

latched it shut, his hands and head poking through.

"Are you supposed to be bent over like that, Philip?"

"Sure, Bruce. It's part of the humiliation."

"Now what do I do?"

"You're supposed to humiliate me."

"How should I do that, Philip?"

"That's up to you, Bruce."

"Alright. Let me think… ah, I've got it!"

Bruce went into the bedroom and returned with a fishing tackle box.

"You're gonna fish me?"

"No, this is my ex-wife's old makeup she left behind."

"What are you gonna do with that?"

"I'm going to put it on your face and make you a pretty lady."

"That's pretty humiliating, Bruce."

"Say, hold on a minute, Philip—I just had the most fabulous idea!"

The Fury was the only vehicle traveling the Ocean Parkway on this Tuesday evening, just before midnight, windows down, salt air whipping through the cabin, autumn moon Waxing Gibbous over the Atlantic, surf crashing, engine gurgling.

Just east of the Jones Beach Field 6 parking lot, Philip Jr. made a U-Turn and pulled into the overgrowth of beach grass and bayberry plants next to Zachs Bay. Slowly he maneuvered the vehicle through a patch of small evergreens and parked in a clearing not visible from road or beach.

From the trunk he removed a shovel and two Kingsford

charcoal briquet bags, the tops of each of the heavy paper receptacles rolled closed at the top. Ten feet from the car he started digging until he reached wet sand four feet down. He unrolled the first bag and dumped it, fine ash fleeing with the breeze as the heavier stuff fell into the hole, then folded it into a square and dropped it in. He did the same with the second bag, then refilled the hole with the backfill and a few shovelfuls from random nearby spots. When it was filled he walked on it and kept adding dirt until it felt compact and flat, then, with his foot, swept sand and pine needles over the entire area until he could no longer tell where the hole had been.

Wearing knockoff Nina Ricci sunglasses, chain-smoking Kent Golden Lights 100s, Joyce painted long into the night, as she'd done the night before, and the night before that, surrounded by newsprint pages on the floor splattered with oil paint, mostly reds and blacks, one of them a copy of *The Village Voice* open to the art gallery advertisements, in the lower right corner a black rectangle ad with cutout text—

The Madame Shazbot Gallery
at 16 Jones Street
presents
"The Aborted",
a new collection of paintings
by emerging artist
Joyce Smith.
November 13
7:00 PM

In the parking lot of St. Agnes Catholic Church in Centereach, Suffolk County, the annual Autumnal Craft Fair about to begin, Bruce and Philip unloaded from the trunk of Bruce's unmarked cruiser the boxes of crafts they'd earlier retrieved from Philip's basement onto a Radio Flyer wagon.

"I'm still not sure this is such a hot idea, Bruce."

"Philip, stop. This idea is scorching and you look divine. Hold on, there's some lipstick on your teeth."

"What if someone recognizes me?"

"No one will ever recognize you in that wig."

"I still think we should have gone with the blond one. A redhead might be a little too burlesque for this crowd. Are you sure no one's gonna recognize me?"

"Philip, we're in a place called Centereach. Who the hell's ever heard of Centereach, for God's sake? Though I do like the name. And I'll be doing all the talking, and you'll just be standing there next to the merchandise like one of the showgirls on *Let's Make a Deal*. I'll tell everyone you're my wife and you have laryngitis and are under doctor's orders not to speak, and that you made everything, and, if anyone asks, I'll say we're from Delaware."

"What part of Delaware are we from, Bruce?"

"It doesn't matter, Philip, I'll be doing all the talking."

"We took the kids down to Bethany Beach once, it was pretty nice. But I still don't know about this dress, Bruce. The ladies at our church don't wear dresses this short."

"Do you really want to look like one of those old bags at church, Philip?"

"Well, no, Bruce, but this seems like a lotta leg for a craft fair."

"Exactly, Philip. If these old bags bring their randy old husbands and you're standing there looking like Lucille Ball, these things will sell like hotcakes."

Dozing in the small break area at the back of Helga's Beauty Parlor, Joyce was awakened by her coworker, Lottie.

"Joyce! What the hell?"

"Huh? What?"

"Mrs. Stevenson fell asleep under the hood and her timer went off almost an hour ago!"

"What?"

"The perm rods just started falling onto her lap! The solution burned her hair off!"

Helga Bridgewater, iron-haired beauty parlor owner, came in, arms folded.

"Lottie, go take care of Mrs. Stevenson, while I have a chat with Ms. Smith. Tell her we won't charge her for the appointment and don't stop apologizing. Give her a drink if she'll take one. There's a bottle of Four Roses and some blackberry brandy under the cash register."

Ms. Bridgewater lit a long cigarette and took a drag. She exhaled, then, in deep smoker's voice, "Joyce, I need you to tell me the truth, dear. Are you stoned on drugs?"

"No, of course not!"

"Well, dear, that's what all the druggies say. But you and I know the truth, Joyce. You need help. Professional help. I've seen this before and I know exactly what to do. I'm going to give you time off so you can go to a rehabilitation facility. There's a good one in Rocky Point, out in Suffolk County. Then, after you get clean, I will welcome you back with open arms."

"But I'm not a druggie, Ms. Bridgewater. I'm an artist."

"All artists are druggies, dear. Everyone knows that."

Oscar, fingers in chain links, was watching the workers and trucks and machinery down in the construction pit, where two enormous squares were sprouting from the bedrock, when a man in an orange vest and scuffed white hardhat, holding two hot dogs with sauerkraut and a bottle of Yoo-hoo, joined him at the fence.

"The Egyptians had their pyramids," he said, "and we're gonna have ours. When you're up there, it'll be like standing on top of the world."

In an Istanbul alley, the trio of Americans—Dick Ritter in yellow Hawaiian shirt and Pittsburgh Pirates cap, C.T. Griffey in orange Hawaiian shirt and San Diego Padres cap, and Roger Ramsey in red Hawaiian shirt and Detroit Tigers home cap—stopped at the door of a crumbling three-story building with dozens of frayed wires hanging from an awkwardly leaning pole on the roof.

Dick knocked, and, almost immediately, the door was pushed open by a large bald man with a thick mustache, who nodded and stepped aside.

Inside smelled of fried lamb intestines, Tekel cigarettes, and hashish. They went up two flights of stairs to another door. Dick knocked and it was opened by a cigarette girl in a belly dancer costume.

"Do you have any Viceroy 100s?" Roger asked, digging in the pocket of his Levi's. "These Turkish cigarettes are hurting my lungs."

"Yes," she said, handing him a pack and taking his lira. She then led them to the hostess lectern outside the waiting room, where they were greeted by an aged woman dressed in black silks, her hair poorly dyed black, in front of her a long brown cigarette burning in a gold ashtray.

"Hey, Madame Gün," Dick said. "We got three tonight, and Roger's with us, so you know what that means."

"If it isn't the American *tourists* on their three-year vacation," she said, her voice deeper than theirs, "including tall and handsome with the schoolgirl fetish. We are crowded tonight, so take a seat at the hookah bar, and be careful, darlings, visibility is low this evening."

Moments later at the hookah bar—

"So, what are you guys thinking about doing after the service?" Dick asked.

"I'm going to flight school to get a helicopter pilot license," C.T. said.

"Flight school? If you wanted to fly, numb nuts, then why the hell didn't you join the Air Force? They'd have taught you that crap for free."

"I didn't know what I wanted to do back when my guidance counselor told me about this program. But all the time I've spent here staring off at nothing has given me time to think, and now I know that's what I want to do. What about you?"

"I'm gonna open a nightclub in Hawaii."

"What kind of nightclub?"

"One with booze and girls."

"Sweet. I'll fly over and visit when I get my chopper."

"You can't fly a helicopter from the mainland to Hawaii, Lindbergh."

"Shoot. Well, maybe I'll open a chopper business in Hawaii and fly tourists around."

"Yeah, good luck with that one, pal. What about you, Roger?"

"I don't know, I haven't really thought about it."

"What the hell do you think about all day?"

"Uh, I don't know. Beer ads. Girls. Baseball. Football. Trains. Joyce. White Castle."

"Love those little hamburgers," C.T. said.

"Hey, Roger, I know what would be good for you."

"Private investigator?" C.T. suggested.

"P.I.? You really think Big Spanky here would make a good private dick? Maybe you could fly him around in your chopper while he's working on cases."

"I like that idea," Roger said.

"I don't," Dick said. "You'd be in way over your head. My friend Toothpick works with a lot of private dicks and trust me, pal, you ain't the type. But I do know what would be perfect for you. I was talking to this guy the other day whose brother is a U.S. Customs Agent. He says the job's a piece of cake. You get to hang out at the airport all day and go through people's luggage and play with the drug sniffing dogs, and you get tons of cigarette breaks, and a gun, and, after twenty years, you retire with a big fat pension."

"You get to play with the dogs?"

"Sure."

"Wow."

They'd been at the hookah bar an hour when a woman wearing a Fenerbahçe S.K. kit fashioned with cheerleader spankies and pom poms made of strips cut from *The Hürriyet Daily News* appeared through the fog calling, "Mr. Roger? Mr. Roger?"

"You're up, Mister Customs Man," Dick said, slapping Roger on the shoulder, then calling out, "Hey, sweetheart, over here."

On Canal Street, Oscar stopped at the door of a graffiti-covered three-story building and reached for the handle, but pulled his hand away at the last second.

He looked up at a crow sitting on the roof ledge, then down at his stomach. Again he reached for the door and this time opened it.

Inside smelled of rice and cigarettes. He looked up the stairs, then again down at his stomach.

"You're doing this," he said, taking a deep breath, feeling the sweaty bills in his pocket.

He ascended the two flights and proceeded cautiously down the corridor. The door to the Wellness Clinic was at the far end.

He knocked and the peephole dimmed.

"I'm here to see Doctor Wu about the ancient Chinese weight loss remedy," he said.

"The line is all the way down the block," said Glenda, gallery assistant, at the second floor window of Madame Shazbot's office. "And did you see that dress she's wearing? It looks like she ordered it from the Sears catalog. They're gonna eat her alive."

The Madame lifted the lid of a small wooden box on her desk and took out a long brown cigarette.

"That's what I'm counting on," she said, smirking, as Glenda lit her cigarette.

Jasmine opened her eyes and looked around.

"What?" she groaned. She tried to move, then began screaming when she realized she was nude and tied to a ping pong table.

"That's enough now," said a male voice. "You're in God's house, and He doesn't like screaming. Besides, no one will hear you down here."

"Where am I?"

"In the basement."

"Who are you?"

"I am a servant of Our Lord, Jesus Christ, Savior."

"God, help me! Help me! Hellllllllp!"

"God isn't going to help you if you continue to scream in His house." The man stepped into the light, nude except for a weathered clerical collar, young, tall, bony, thick glasses, brown bowl haircut. "If you don't stop, I'll have no choice but to cut off one of your toes. I have God's permission."

She stopped screaming, but was still breathing heavily.

"What do you want with me?"

"I don't want anything from you. I'm merely doing God's work."

"What are you gonna do to me?"

"Whatever He tells me to do to you."

Joyce squirted the burning briquets with the can of Wizard Charcoal Lighter Fluid until the flames in the barbecue at the end of the driveway were as high as the canvas awning covering the back patio.

Into the fire she tossed the bundle of letters forwarded by Madame Shazbot, many of them death threats from women's libbers, and a few encouraging ones from new age religious groups such as *The New New New Crusaders* and *The Purple Lifers of the Christian Sage.*

Next she tossed in the newspaper clippings, among them a review from *The Village Voice* with the headline "Plain Jane Pro-Lifer Unleashes Agenda on Stunned West Village Audience", another from *The Village Green Preservation Society Newsletter* titled "Another Morbid Showing at Madame Shazbot's", and one from *Newsday*, "West Hempstead Artist Draws Large Crowd at Manhattan Gallery".

Finally she picked up the first of the nineteen oil canvases stacked beside her and put it on the barbecue and watched it burn center outward, the oils making the fire hotter and redder and darker, until there was nothing left but frame, which she broke into pieces and tossed onto the coals.

It was breezy, the tower of flame swirling ever closer to the awning, until a gust brought fire to fabric and it started to burn.

Unaware, she was smoking a cigarette and watching the fourth canvas burn when someone behind her started shouting, "Fire! Fire! Fire!"

Running towards her up the driveway was a bald, overweight, high school-age kid with no hair whatsoever, not even eyebrows.

"Oh my God... Oscar? Is that you?"

"Jeez, Rog, you look awful," Dick said.

"You do, Rog," C.T. added.

"When was the last time you stepped on a scale?"

"When the last one broke."

"And when was the last time you went to the dentist? I can barely see your teeth behind all that gunk."

"I haven't been to the dentist."

"Since you've been here?"

"Since Mommy and Daddy died."

"We gotta get you cleaned up," Dick said. "If you don't do something now, that little lady of yours back home will drop you faster than a sack of turds. But don't worry, pal, I know just the guy who can get you whipped into shape."

In the kitchen of the Smith house—

"Philip, will you please try to relax? Please?"

"I'm sorry, Bruce. I'm still a little nervous that one of the kids will come home."

"You yourself said Philip Jr. would be out at job interviews all day and Joyce was starting her new job and Oscar doesn't get home until three o'clock. And, besides, Philip, this is a Men in Uniform Brunch. What would they see? Their strapping father in his crisp Navy whites? Me in my old patrolman's uniform? A firefighter? A construction worker?"

"What about the guy in the Indian headdress? And the cowboy with the funny pants?"

"Those are chaps and they are part of a cowboy's uniform, just like the headdress is part of an Indian's uniform. I was actually thinking of getting a pair myself. Now please, Philip, don't ruin this for me. I worked hard on this brunch and I want it to be perfect, so please go out there, have a couple of mimosas, and try to enjoy yourself."

"Okay, Bruce. I promise I'll try to relax."

Through the Beetle windshield she looked across the shopping center parking lot at the script lettering on the sign for Mr. Louie's Beauty Parlor, then at her watch. The engine was off and her keys were in her purse and her hand was on the door handle, but it refused to pull.

She took the keys out and put the VW one in the ignition and turned the radio on. She listened to "Down on the Corner", then again looked at her watch.

"Oh well, two minutes late," she said. "Like Daddy says, *You can't be late on the first day, they'll never let you forget it.*"

She pressed the clutch and turned the key and the engine sputtered to life. Slowly she navigated out of the parking lot onto Merrick Road, and, eventually, to Sunrise Highway, heading west.

She pulled into a diner in Valley Stream and bought a copy of *Newsday* from the newspaper machine out front and a pack of Kent Golden Lights 100s from the cigarette machine in the lobby. She was seated at a booth overlooking Sunrise and ordered coffee, scrambled eggs, toast, and bacon.

She opened the *Newsday* to the help wanted classifieds

and looked at a few ads, then closed it and pushed it away. She stared at the traffic until the waitress came back with the coffee, then lit a cigarette.

After she was done eating, she again opened the classifieds, but closed them without looking at any ads. She smoked four more cigarettes, then, leaving the newspaper and a quarter on the table, slid out of the booth and paid the bill at the register.

Back in West Hempstead, she turned the Beetle onto Morton Avenue and encountered two unfamiliar cars parked in the driveway behind her father's cruiser, and several more parked on the street in front of the house.

"What the hell?" she asked, driving by, then parking in front of the house next door.

In an industrial zone outside of Istanbul, the interior of Bull's Boxing Gym was thick with smoke, not only from smokers, but also from machines pumping tobacco and hashish smoke into the building to emulate ring conditions in clubs and arenas throughout the country.

The trio of Hawaiian-shirted American tourists approached the very large proprietor of the establishment, a hairless man except for the bushy mustache and sideburns.

"So, this is fat American you tell me about," Bull said to Dick. "This will be long project."

"That's alright, Curly. We've got six months to whip this guy into shape so he can go back to the States and marry his little lady."

"This will cost you. And do not call me 'Curly'."

"I don't know about this," Roger said in Dick's ear.

"What? You're gonna chicken out? Don't you wanna go back home and marry Joyce and become a Customs Inspector?"

"Right now I just want a beer."

"Ha," Bull laughed. "Typical weak American. But, if you are serious, I can whip him into shape better than your American Army."

"We're not Army, Short-Pants," Dick said.

"Right, I forget, you are American *tourists*. Ha! And if you call me 'Short-Pants' again, I will bull charge you to other side of gym. Now, back to business, we also have dentist chair in upstairs office, Dr. Luigi here three mornings a week. He is also proctologist if you are in need of such services."

Roger looked at the exit.

"I'll tell you what, Rog," Dick said, pulling him aside. "Before you start training, we'll throw you the greatest party ever. My buddy Toothpick in Honolulu can have some real cheerleader uniforms flown in from Moanalua High, and maybe even a few cheerleaders. And I'll even sweeten the pot. It won't be just a party, it'll be a three-day bender. And then we'll turn you over to Yul Brynner over there and he'll whip you into shape so you don't go back home looking like the Goodyear Blimp with bad teeth. Do we have a deal, champ?"

It was after 2:00 am.

Philip Jr.'s bed was empty. Across the hall, the space beneath Joyce's door was finally dark.

Downstairs, Oscar heard his father snoring through the closed bedroom door.

The night was dark, only a blur of moonlight filtering

through the clouds, but his eyes adjusted quickly as he crossed the dewy backyard lawn, pajama pant cuffs soaked, bare feet sprinkled with grass blades, to the old apple tree in the corner.

From behind the bushes next to the fence he retrieved his father's old wooden folding ladder and a coil of rope.

Beneath the tree branch from which a rope swing once hung, he opened the ladder, then, coil over shoulder, climbed, securing the rope around the branch and the noose around his neck.

With a photograph of his mother in hand, he sat on the top step and cried.

The ladder began to creak and wobble. He tried to steady himself, but the movement caused one of the legs to snap and the ladder to fall over.

He felt a moment of freefall, then a tug on his neck when the rope snapped. He hit the grass hard, twisting his ankle and landing on his side next to the broken ladder.

Above him, the branch creaked loudly, then broke and fell, landing on top of him, breaking the femur of his already injured leg, and knocking him unconscious.

At Gate 8 inside the TWA terminal at JFK, Joyce lit another cigarette and watched the deplaning passengers emerge from the jetway until the last one appeared, a tall, fit, handsome man wearing a red Hawaiian shirt, jeans, sunglasses, and a baseball cap.

"Did the idiot miss his flight?" she asked herself, looking around.

The man was approaching, but she continued looking

around until he was right in front of her.

"Hello there," she said. "Oh, maybe you can help me. I saw that you were on that flight and was wondering if you happened to notice if anyone was left... wait... Roger? Is that you behind those glasses?"

"Hello, Joyce."

"Oh my God... Roger, wow... it looks like you were on vacation."

"I can't talk about it, Joyce. Are you gonna kiss me?"

"Yes, sure."

She kissed him uncertainly, then said, "Well, uh, I was thinking you probably want to go to White Castle?"

His nose twitched.

"Roger? Are you going to take those sunglasses off? It's dark out."

"No. Let's go to White Castle."

Behind the wheel of the Beetle, stopped at a red light, Joyce looked at Roger, still wearing the sunglasses, sitting stiffly.

"Are you okay, Roger? Did something happen to you over there? I mean, you look great, really, really great, but you're being quiet and mysterious."

"I'm fine. Let's get to White Castle."

At their booth, a tray of heavily onioned little hamburgers between them, Joyce reached across the table and removed Roger's sunglasses.

"Wow, Roger. You look good. Really, really good."

"You keep saying that."

"Well, it's just so—shocking—how good you look."

"I have something important to tell you."

"You do?"

"Yes."

"Well, what is it?"

"I'm going to be a man in uniform."

"Wait—what?"

"I'm going to be a U.S. Customs Inspector."

"Oh. You're gonna work at the post office?"

"No, at the airport. Checking passports. Going through people's luggage. Playing with the dogs."

"The dogs?"

"The ones that sniff for illegal drugs."

"Oh, wow, that sounds—interesting."

"I need to know, Joyce."

"Need to know what?"

"If you'll marry me."

"Oh. Well, Roger, seeing how good you look, like a TV star, and that you've found some sort of job, wow, I guess, I mean, sure, I guess."

"I love you, Joyce."

"I love you too."

They kissed across the table.

"These burgers smell good," Roger said.

"Well, have one."

He picked up a burger and took a bite. He moaned as he chewed and stuffed the rest of it into his mouth, then, bun bits falling from lips, reached for another.

"We should get some beers after this," he said, mouth full.

In a tenement basement on West 115th Street, Clyde listened to Zola tell of the Plymouth Fury she'd just seen on Morningside Avenue.

"And you're sure it's the same one you saw Tafari get

into?"

"Same driver too, white minister with glasses."

"Dumbass motherfucker. Alright, go to the corner and get his attention if he drives by again. I'll be right behind you."

In the ladies' room at Trinity Lutheran, the dress rehearsal having just wrapped up, Joyce, leaning against a sink, was starting to cry when the door opened and Dolly came in.

"Oh, sweetheart, what's wrong?" she asked, hurrying over.

"I don't know if I want to marry Roger."

"Oh, honey, it's normal to feel that way before your wedding."

"It's not just today. It's this feeling I get lately when I'm with him. It feels like he's a ten year old and I'm his mother. I always have to tell him what to do and what not to do. He never thinks to do anything himself. It's like he's a man-child."

"Well, that's understandable when you consider he was raised by that lush sister of his, if that's what you want to call what she did. But don't worry, sweetheart, he'll grow out of it."

"How did he not grow out of it in the Army?"

"Because he was surrounded by a bunch of immature boys just like him, and now he needs a real woman like you to help him become a real man. Besides, I thought you liked his boyish charm. But, if that's not what you want, maybe you need a man more like my Freddy."

Heading up Morningside Avenue, approaching West 115th, half the streetlights out and the park to the left invisible in the darkness, he pulled the Fury next to the curb and waited for the woman to approach the open passenger side window.

"Lookin' for a good time, Padre?" she asked, leaning in.

"Yes," he smiled. "I do happen to be looking for some guilty pleasures this evening."

"Joyce, do you, in the name of God and Our Savior, Jesus Christ, take Roger to be your lawfully wedded husband, to honor and obey from this day forward, for better or for worse, for richer or for poorer, in sickness and in health, until death do you part?"

"…"

"Joyce?"

Peripherally, she could see the orange of Dolly's hair and the blue of Fred's sharkskin suit.

"I do."

In the men's room of American Legion Hall Post 1087, where Bruce was adjusting Philip's cumber bunt—

"Sure, the kid's a flake," Philip said, "but it's not like him to just not show up, especially to his sister's wedding, and now the reception."

"Maybe his car broke down?"

"It's a five minute walk from the house."

"When was the last time you saw him again?"

"A few days ago, at the house. I reminded him about the wedding, but then I've been busy planning this thing. We don't see each other much anyway, I go to work early and he's out all day looking for a job."

"Maybe he finally got a job and he had to start right away?"

"On a Saturday?"

"Alright, maybe not that, but I'm sure everything's fine. You're just getting worked up because you're a cop and you've seen bad things and it's making you worried."

"I hope you're right, Bruce. But I have that bad feeling. You know the one I'm talking about."

"I do, Philip. But, for your daughter's sake, please try to enjoy the reception, and hopefully at some point he'll show up. If he doesn't, we'll worry about it later."

Joyce, alone at the bar while the bartender was fetching another bottle of red wine, was startled by the gravelly voice in her ear.

"It's not too late," Fred said. "My Caddy's parked in the lot. Plenty of room in the back if you want to experience a real man before you run off with that clown."

They looked at Roger, the bowtie of his powder blue tux undone, wearing ditty-bop shades, he and his Army buddies, Dick and C.T., dancing drunkenly in front of the band playing "Louie Louie."

"I thought he was your friend."

"If he was my friend, he would have stepped aside and let

me have you."

"Do you guys know 'Wildwood Days'?" Dolly asked the lead singer/bassist of The Hempstead Turnpike Experience.

"We don't do Bobby Darin," he answered into the microphone.

"It's not Bobby Darin, moron, it's Bobby Rydell!"

"Who?"

"What kind of musicians are you that you've never heard of Bobby Rydell?"

"Uh, cool ones."

"I'm going down to the station," Philip said to Bruce.

"Philip, maybe you should wait until morning, when you're rested."

"I'm going now, Bruce. This is my son we're talking about here."

"I'm sorry, Philip. You're right. But please let me drive, you've had a bit too much to drink."

"I'm fine, Bruce."

Leaning against the Cadillac, Rich Richards, drummer for The Hempstead Turnpike Experience, chuckled as he passed the joint to guitarist Greg Greening.

"Check it out," he said, looking at the overweight man

with the large redheaded woman they'd encountered earlier exiting the Legion Hall.

"Wait here," they heard the man say to the woman.

"Uh-oh, here he comes," said lead singer/bassist, Robbi Timothi.

The man stopped in front of them and lit a Winston.

"You guys comfortable?" he asked.

"Sure," Timothi responded. "Why? Is this your car, Ralph Kramden?"

"It is my car."

"Wow, I didn't know Ralph Kramden could afford a Cadillac on that bus driver's salary," Greening laughed.

"Looks like Alice over there put on some weight," Richards chuckled

"Say, Ralphie Boy," said Timothi, mimicking Ed Norton, "Alice is looking a little lonely over there. Why don't you go over and serenade her with some Bobby Rydell?"

The Experience laughed.

The man took a drag from the cigarette and flicked it away, then grabbed Richards and Greening by the back of their afro-perms and smashed their faces against the trunk. Several of their teeth rattled off the back of the car and their noses were gushing blood as they dropped to the asphalt.

"Please don't hurt me," Timothi begged, hands up, stepping away.

"I'll make you a deal," the man said. "If you go over there and sing 'Wildwood Days' to my wife without messing up any of the words, I'll let it slide. But if you mess up just one word, or hit one bad note, you're gonna look like your buddies there."

"Ugh," said Captain Mueller, looking away from the body fished out of the East River earlier that morning, male, Caucasian, early twenties, wearing a clerical uniform, the word "MURDERER" carved into his forehead, his testicles having fallen out of his mouth when they pulled off the duct tape covering it.

"I haven't seen anything like this since I was in the mob," said Detective Fisch.

"Any leads?"

"The guys on the boat think it came from upriver, possibly Harlem or the Bronx. But nothing else."

"Alright, let's figure out who this guy is, then we'll take it from there."

In the maternity ward waiting room at Mercy Hospital, Roger reached beneath his chair and retrieved another can of Budweiser from the Styrofoam cooler, then lit another Viceroy 100 and resumed staring up at the television mounted on the wall tuned to the WPIX Channel 11 News—

"…The landmark Supreme Court decision will make abortion a Constitutional Right in the United States. And now here's Don with sports…"

"Ramsey… Roger Ramsey…"

"Here!" he said, raising his hand at the nurse with the clipboard standing at the doorway.

"Room 301, Ramsey."

"Be there in a minute."

The nurse went away and Roger looked back up at the television, finishing his beer and cigarette during the commercial break and waiting for the out-of-town basketball and hockey scores before getting up.

In room 301, Griffin Archibald Ramsey looked at his mother and frowned.

"Why is he looking at me like that?" the mother asked Nurse O'Meara.

"It's probably just gas."

"He looks annoyed."

"Don't worry, dear, it'll pass."

It was well into the darkness of night, after 10:00 pm, when Oscar finally completed his appointed rounds, 478 houses, then squeezed behind the wheel of his mail Jeep and headed back to the post office, where, at this late hour, the only other person there was Earl, the night janitor—

"You don't look too good," he said to Oscar.

"I don't feel too good either."

"Yeah, but you made it through the first day. I've seen guys way more in shape than you quit halfway through their routes on the first day."

"Oh yeah?"

"Sure. But the guys who make it through the first day, especially the big guys like you, they're tough, and they're the ones that make it. Everyone thinks being a mailman is easy, but it ain't no easy feat delivering mail to 500 houses a day, especially with all them goddamn dogs."

In the living room of his and Joyce's one-bedroom apartment in Lynbrook, Roger, on the couch they'd bought at the Salvation Army Store, maneuvered out of the sag his girth had caused the cushion and turned up the volume knob on the television—

"From the Madison Square Garden Bowling Center in Manhattan, New York, I'm Bob Murphy, and this is Bowling for Dollars—"

"Holy cow, it's the announcer for the Mets," he said, lighting a Viceroy 100, sipping his Budweiser.

"Our first contestant this evening is Molly from Malverne, Long Island. Welcome, Molly!"

"Hi, Bob! I'm so excited to be here!"

"That's terrific, Molly. I see you brought your own ball. Do you bowl a lot, Molly?"

"Yes, Bob! We have a cute little underground bowling center in Malverne right next to the train station! In fact, I threw a practice game before I got on the train and came here!"

"Molly, it sounds like you're raring to go, so let's get started. The jackpot ball is $500, but why don't you throw a practice ball first to work out the nerves."

"Sure thing, Bob!"

"Roger?" Joyce called from the kitchen. "Are you going to take out the trash?"

"In a minute," he called back.

"You said that an hour and a half ago, and then an hour ago, and then—"

"I'm watching something."

"You're always watching something."

"Well, Molly, now that you've worked out the nerves, it all comes down to this one shot. Throw a strike and you'll win the $500 jackpot. Are you ready, Molly?"

"I sure am, Bob!"

"I need you to do it now, Roger," Joyce said, stepping in front of the television. "I can't fit anything else into it."

"I'll get to it when I have a chance."

"You've had the last ninety minutes to do it!"

"A slow roller down the right side of the lane... now hooking towards the center... hooking... hooking..."

Roger leaned to the right trying to see around Joyce, but she turned off the TV.

"Goddamnit, Joyce! Why did you do that? Now I'll never know if Molly got a strike! She was from Malverne!"

"You would have known if you'd taken out the trash ninety minutes ago."

Roger's face turned crimson.

"Urrrrrggggghhhharrrrurrr!"

He pushed himself up from the couch and stormed past Joyce, towards the apartment door.

"Where are you going?"

"To the bar, where I can relax in peace!"

"On your way, can you take out—"

He slammed the door behind him.

In the bedroom, the baby started crying.

Stacy Millicent Ramsey looked at her mother and frowned.

"Aw, she has gas," the mother said.

Nurse O'Meara did not respond, distracted was she by the contrast of the pale, dark-haired baby to the freckle-blond mother, and the lack of any resemblance to her unconscious, chestnut-haired father in the waiting room, or the blond-haired brother relentlessly pulling the knobs on the cigarette machine.

"Nurse? It is just gas, right?"

"Oh, yes, dear. That's right. Probably just gas."

In the living room, Griff in the playpen, the television tuned to the CBS sitcom *All in the Family*, his mother in the bedroom feeding his baby sister, his father on the couch—

"Da-da!" the boy exclaimed, pointing at Michael "Meathead" Stivic, liberal son in-law and general nuisance of conservative dock foreman Archie Bunker.

"Holy cow, your first word!" Roger exclaimed, working his way out of the cushion sag and pushing himself up. "Say it again!"

"Da-da," Griff said, again pointing at the television.

"No, I'm Da-da," Roger said, pointing at himself.

"Da-da!" the boy insisted, pointing at Meathead.

Roger turned off the television.

Griff started to cry.

"Me Da-da," Roger said, pointing at himself.

The boy shook his head and cried, "Meathead Da-da!"

"That man isn't your Da-da. I'm your Da-da. Now say it. Who's your Da-da?"

"Meathead!" the boy cried.

"Say Da-da to me."

"No."

"Who am I?"

"Stupid."

"What?"

"Moron."

"How are you learning these words so fast?"

"Idiot."

"Okay, let's try it one more time. Who am I again?"

"Lardass."

Roger turned crimson.

"If you call me a name other than 'Da-da' one more time, you're gonna get your first spanking. Now let's try again. Who am I?"

"Fat Lazy Roger!"

"That's it," Roger said, lifting Griff out of the playpen and putting him over his knee. He pulled down the crying boy's pants and diaper, which was full of wet poop, some of which smeared onto Roger's fingertips and underneath his nails—

"Urrrrrgggggghhhharrrrurrr!" he roared.

"Will your husband be joining us, Mrs. Ramsey?" asked Nancy, the gold-blazered real estate agent, in front of the 1,450 square foot, 3 bedroom 1½ bath house on Oak Street in West Hempstead listed for $35,000, half-block from the shopping center with the Korvette's discount department store and Woolworth, and around the block from her father's house on Morton Avenue.

"No," Joyce said.

Inside was unfurnished and in better condition than the apartment. On the main floor there was a decent sized kitchen, dining room, living room, powder room, and small den.

Upstairs there were three bedrooms and one bathroom. The third floor was a semi-finished attic space, and the basement was unfinished.

"Well, what do you think?" Nancy asked.

"This might work. And it would be nice to have Korvette's and Woolworth right down the block. Is anyone else interested?"

"There is another young couple who seemed to like it. This is one of the few houses in this price range that isn't a total wreck. Do you think your husband will want to see it?"

"Put in an offer of thirty-four thousand," Joyce said.

"What about your husband?"

"Just put in the offer, Nancy."

From the playpen in the apartment living room, Stacy heard the laugh and turned towards the television—

"Ah-ah-ah-ah-ah-ah-ah-ah," laughed Count von Count. *"I will count these candles."*

The Count counted the four "candles", small light bulbs with flame shapes, then subtracted them as they were extinguished, leaving the castle dark.

"Ah-ah-ah," Stacy laughed, tiny fingers clinging to playpen mesh.

In the apartment living room, the television tuned to the CBS sitcom *Good Times*—

"Dy-no-mite!" exclaimed J.J., the oldest of the Evans

children.

"Dy-no-mite!" repeated Griff, he and the audience laughing and applauding.

The German shepherd appeared after Oscar, atop a four-step brick stoop, closed the lid on the mailbox attached to the house.

The yard was fenced with chain link about four feet high, the gates to the driveway and front walk latched shut.

He wasn't a huge dog, but he was growling, showing his teeth, drooling. They stared each other down as Oscar subtly reached into his mailbag and pulled out a small Milk Bone treat.

"Here, boy!" he said, tossing the treat over the dog's head, distracting him long enough to leap off the stoop, sprint to the fence, and hop over it, just before the crazed canine got there.

"See ya, tomorrow, King," he said, tossing another Milk Bone into the yard.

In the den of the house in West Hempstead, the television tuned to the CBS sitcom *The Jeffersons*, Griff on the shag carpet—

"Who you callin' crazy, honky?" George Jefferson asked Tom Willis.

The studio audience howled, as did Griff, and tens of millions more across prime-time America.

"Don't call me honky!" Willis roared, and everyone

laughed again, until he asked George, *"How would you like it if I called you 'nigger'?"*

This time they laughed uncertainly, many gasping, including Griff.

"Welcome aboard, Fred," said Bill Torrey, president of the New York Islanders, adjusting his bowtie, extending his hand to the owner and president of Slate Bulb & Electric, now *The Official Bulb & Lighting Company of the New York Islanders.*

"Thanks, Bill," Fred said, shaking his hand, then lighting a Winston.

"You're joining us at the perfect time. Our young players are gaining valuable playoff experience, and we feel it's only a matter of time before we make it to the next level. Who knows? Maybe we'll even bring Lord Stanley's Cup to Long Island."

"That would be something," Fred said.

"Anyway, Fred, as soon as your marketing team sends us the artwork, we'll get this barn plastered with Slate placards!"

The letter was addressed to Oscar and rubber stamped with the return address for the FDNY exam office.

He brought it upstairs to his room, opened it, then tacked it to the wall next to the other letter stating that he'd passed the written exam, but had failed the Candidate Physical Ability Test.

"Philip, there is absolutely nothing to worry about," Bruce said, fixing Philip's wig of long blond curls, then making an adjustment on his carnation pink dress. "We're in Paris! No one knows us here, and the French don't care."

"I don't know Bruce. There seems to be a lot of Americans here."

"So what? They don't know us. Who do you think is going to recognize us here? We could be Germans for all they know."

"I guess you're right, Bruce. We didn't even recognize anyone on the plane from New York."

"So, you're ready then?"

"I suppose."

"Oh, and don't forget your gloves and parasol. And there's some lipstick on your teeth."

Hand-in-hand they passed through the hotel lobby to the Paris sunshine, where they strolled along the Seine on *Quai de l'Hôtel de ville*, towards The Louvre.

"Isn't this wonderful, Philip?" Bruce asked. "Being out in the open in gay *pa-ree* without a care in the world. And you look pretty in that dress, dear. Don't you feel pretty, Philip?"

"I do feel pretty, Bruce."

The streets were more crowded near the Louvre, and they heard more voices speaking English.

"Maybe we should head back to the hotel now," Philip said. "These heels are doing a number on my ankles."

"Philip, we talked about this. We're going to the Louvre and that's all there is to it. Now let's get on line."

They got on line behind a group of Americans, four couples who appeared to be retirees on vacation. One of them, a man with gray hair cut high and tight and a black mustache, turned around and his eyes widened—

"Holy cow! Bruce Beasley, Fifth Precinct!"

"Oh, hey, Daniels," Bruce said. "It's been a while. Fancy meeting you here."

Daniels then looked at Philip, now wearing a pair of knockoff Nina Ricci sunglasses and looking away.

"Phil?" he asked. "Phil Smith, is that you?"

In the salon of the Flynt mansion on the North Shore—

"What's wrong, sweetheart?" Dolly asked, pulling a Virginia Slim 100 from her cigarette case and lighting it.

"Nothing," Joyce said, lighting a Kent Golden Light 100, sipping zinfandel. "Roger."

"Is he cheating?"

"No. I don't think so. It's not that. It's just him. He's never going to change. He's just going to keep getting gradually worse until—I don't know—he dies?"

"Do you want me to set something up with Madame Zoë? My treat?"

"Uh, thanks, Doll, but I think I'll pass on that one."

"Well, let me know if you ever change your mind."

"I need *something* to change, or else I'm gonna go crazy. I do everything around the house and take care of the kids by myself. He comes home every night and expects warm dinner on the table and won't let us speak to him until he's done eating and lights his cigarette. And then he sits in front of the TV all night drinking beer and watching some stupid game. And there's always some stupid game. And he's cheap. And fat. And I have no reason to believe that any of this is ever gonna change."

"Jeez, Joyce, if you're sure you don't need Madame Zoë, you at least need a night out. You guys should come to an Islander game with us. We have season tickets and our own luxury box at the Coliseum—"

"Ugh."

"Wait, I have a better idea! Last year, Fred did the new lighting at Studio 54 and became friends with the owner, and he told him he could bring me and a couple of friends. That's what we should do! Did you know that Sylvester Stallone hangs out there? And Burt Reynolds?"

"Burt Reynolds?"

"Sure! And tons of other celebrities!"

"That sounds fun, but it's probably a little out of our price range."

"Nonsense! The whole night will be on us, and I won't take 'no' for an answer. We can even be like movie stars and hire a limousine to take us all into the City together—"

"Umm, it would probably be better if we just met you there," Joyce said, stamping out her cigarette.

It was just after midnight, the Cape Cod style house engulfed in flames, a boy and a girl at each of the upstairs windows screaming for help, when the wailing truck from the West Hempstead Fire Department pulled up and the volunteers, led by Oscar, started jumping off before it had come to a stop.

In mask and tank, ax in hand, he ran to the front door and attacked the handle until it fell off and the door swung open. He raced through the flames blocking the staircase and up to the girl's room just as the guys outside had gotten the ladder to the window, which Wilson was climbing. Oscar helped her out the window onto Wilson's back, then ran into the boy's room and carried him to his sister's window and handed him off to Wilson, who'd already left the girl with someone below. He then retrieved the wailing, obese cat in the corner and climbed out the window and down the ladder, where the EMS workers were on the lawn assisting the children and their parents, who'd escaped through their first floor bedroom window.

In a matter of minutes, the top floor no longer existed. A short time later, all that remained of the house were pieces of the blackened frame.

Later, at the station, where the guys, too amped to go home, were hanging out, many drinking cans of Piels beer, Captain Rawley called Oscar, who was drinking Welch's white grape juice, into his office.

"Hell of a job, Smith," he said, feet on desk, puffing a Dutch Masters cigar. "I'm gonna make sure my report leaves no doubt that you've got the stuff, and I'm gonna make sure everyone I know at FDNY hears about what you did tonight."

"I can't believe we're really here!" Dolly exclaimed, after she and Fred had met Joyce and Roger outside, where the line to get in was around the block, but Fred said something to the bouncer and they were allowed right in. "I heard that even Bobby Rydell can't get into this place!"

"Wait until you see the lighting," Fred said to Roger.

"I hope Sylvester Stallone is here!" Dolly exclaimed. "And John Travolta!"

On their way to the bar, the foursome encountered several

people who exclaimed, "Hey, Light Bulb Guy!" The bartender greeted Fred as "Mr. Flynt" and said all drinks for he and his party would be on the house.

"I heard that Warhol and Dalí sometimes hang out here," Joyce said to Dolly over the loud music, "Boogie Wonderland".

"What's that, sweetie?" Dolly asked, looking around.

"I heard that Warhol and Dalí sometimes hang out here."

"No, this is my first time here."

"No, I'm talking about Andy Warhol and Salvador Dalí. They sometimes hang out here."

"Who's Salvatore?"

Roger suddenly pointed and exclaimed, "Hey, it's Reggie Jackson!" He then cupped his mouth and shouted towards the Yankee slugger, "Hey, Reggie, let's go Mets!"

Jackson, in black tux and signature metal frames, looked at Roger, then turned to Farrah Fawcett next to him and said, "Yeah, fatso over there can go with the Mets right to last place. Mazzilli is the only Met who can even get in here."

"Is Lee here?" Fawcett asked, looking around.

By eleven, Roger was loaded and Joyce was yawning. Fred and Dolly were talking to the owner and some other people who weren't famous.

"Maybe we should take the next train home," Joyce said in Roger's ear.

"I want to stay."

"Alright, Roger. One more beer."

"Two more beers."

"Fine. Two more beers. Then we're going."

Several minutes later, Roger headed for the men's room, leaving Joyce alone at the bar gazing at the sea of humanity on the dance floor, but no one she recognized, only a few faces that looked vaguely familiar. So tired was she that she didn't notice Fred break from his group and disappear into the crowd until he was beside her.

"Had enough of Roger yet?" he asked in her ear, his gravelly voice now gurgling, his hot breath in her lobe.

"Fred!" she gasped, then started looking around.

"He's not here," Fred said. "He's probably in the bathroom puking on himself."

She tried to get away, but he grabbed her upper arm and tightened his grip the harder she struggled.

Atop a white steed clopping across the dance floor—

"Over there, Mick! A damsel in distress!" cried Andy, seated behind him, arms around his waist.

"I see her, Andy!" said Mick, at the reigns, steering the horse towards the bar.

The crowd dispersed as the steed approached, until it arrived at the end of the bar, where the large man had hold of the damsel's upper arm.

"Let her go, Light Bulb Guy!" Mick ordered, elevated Mockney.

"Yes! You let her go, you, you, Mister Meanie!" Andy demanded, pointing, palms sweating, hair awry, glasses slipping off nose.

Mick extended his hand to the damsel.

"Come with us, Miss," he said.

The man released his grip on the damsel's arm, and Andy joined the effort to pull her atop the horse. Mick then turned the steed around and steered it back to the middle of the dance floor, where they were swarmed by celebrities—Sylvester, John, Burt, Farrah, Reggie, Mazz, Jack, Liza,

Truman, Cher, Brooke, Michael, Diana, Salvador, and the rest—cheering, waving, dancing.

"The seventies are almost over," said television screenwriter and producer Donald P. Bellisario, creator of *Battlestar Galactica*. "People don't want another *Barnaby Jones* or *Cannon*. They want someone cool, hip. A man that male viewers want to be, and female viewers want to be with."

This was inside the office of CBS Network Entertainment President John Backe—pronounced "BOCK-ee", former Air Force fighter pilot turned network executive who'd made a name for himself with bold prime-time programming decisions—during a pitch meeting with Bellisario and Glen A. Larson—co-creator of the popular *Quincy, M.E.* starring Jack Klugman as a Los Angeles County coroner, and who had also worked with Bellisario on *Battlestar*—on the 38th floor of "Black Rock", the CBS building on West 52nd Street in Manhattan.

Backe leaned back in his chair and looked at the rectangle of fluorescent light above him.

"Let me get this straight," he said. "The show is set in Hawaii, and the lead is a former veteran of what again? Something about Army soldiers in Turkey spying on the Soviets?"

"We changed that," Larson said. "They're Vietnam veterans, and the lead and his two buddies are Navy."

"Vietnam veterans, that's pretty bold," Backe said. "But I still don't understand this thing about him driving around in a Ferrari 'thinking out loud', which sounds a lot like talking to oneself. And he's solving mysteries as a Private Investigator, but he's also the security guard on the estate of a reclusive novelist?"

"Yes," Bellisario said. "He's a bachelor in paradise living the life that every schlub in America would want to live. The thinking out loud is a way to bring them in deeper, and enable them to live vicariously through Thomas Magnum, who drives around in a Ferrari solving crimes, who frequents the King Kamehameha Club, who is constantly surrounded by beautiful women, who drinks German beer from longneck bottles, who takes a swim every morning in the tidal pool, who carries a gun in the back of his shorts, who plays pickup basketball on public courts in Waikiki. They'll all want to be this guy."

"And one of the buddies is a black man who owns his own helicopter tour business," Larson added.

"A black business owner? That's George Jefferson bold."

"He's a big strong guy, a badass. And the other buddy is the manager of the King Kamehameha Club, which is sort of like a country club, and he's kind of a smartass, but he's got all sorts of underworld connections that Magnum can tap into, and he's always got a pretty girl on each arm."

"We also put in a running sub-plot where Magnum believes that Higgins, the estate keeper for the reclusive novelist, is actually the novelist himself pretending to be the estate keeper. So it's like he's hiding in plain sight."

"This part sounds a little too Pynchonian to me. I hope you don't tell me next that the guy is going to jump out a window when photographers start climbing out of the toilets trying to snap his picture. That kind of crap might fly on ABC and NBC, but this is CBS, gentlemen."

"No, no, nothing like that. It's more like *The Odd Couple*, there for comic relief. The estate keeper is a stuffy, proper, neat freak like Felix, and Magnum is a freewheeling, beer-drinking sports guy like Oscar."

"I do enjoy comic relief," Backe said. "Do you have the pilot script?"

"Yes, I have it right here," said Bellisario, opening the attaché case on his lap.

"We don't need no education!" the sixth graders bellowed out the windows at the back of the school bus as it pulled to a stop in front of Cornwell Avenue Elementary.

Griff, at the front of the bus with the younger kids, turned and watched the big kids in the back, several of the boys wearing black rock & roll t-shirts that said *Led Zeppelin, Black Sabbath, AC/DC,* and one wearing a white shirt featuring a whitebrick design, upon which, in scrawl that appeared to be blood, *Pink Floyd The Wall.*

Oscar leapt up the stoop, dropped the mail in the box, tossed the Milk Bone to the Doberman charging at him from the driveway, leapt back down, ran across the front lawn, hurdled the fence, then outran the rest of the dogs along his appointed rounds, by the end of which, kids from all over the neighborhood were running with him, sprinting the last stretch to the Post Office, arms raised in triumph, kids cheering, mail Jeeps honking, someone in a passing vehicle on Hempstead Avenue shouting out an open window, "Go get 'em, Oscar!"

At the Korvette's discount department store *Going Out of Business Sale*, frenzied shoppers sorted through quarter-full bins and clothing racks, including Griff's mother, paying no attention to him or Stacy, who was by herself in the Stationery Department, while he was in the Record & Tape Department holding the double-album length cassette in hand, the simple whitebrick cover with blood scrawl text, *Pink Floyd The Wall*, CBS/Columbia Records, and not a security guard in sight, making it easy to slide down his *Superman* Underoos without anyone noticing.

In the Stationery Department, the only colors left in the bin of textured cover pocket journals were the ugly ones, olive green, attaché brown, concrete gray, yet, Stacy and an old lady who smelled like mothballs continued sifting through it, finding only more of the same below, until the eyes of both caught, at the very bottom, a flash of textured crimson.

The old lady reached for it, but Stacy was quicker, snatching the journal from beneath the wrinkled hand, their eyes meeting across the bin.

"Young lady, I saw that journal first, so please be a good little girl and hand it over."

Stacy shook her head.

"Young lady, it is disrespectful to refuse an elder. Now hand me that journal!"

Journal in hand, Stacy ran from the bin and ducked into a circular rack of unsold Botany 500 *Monty Hall Collection* plaid sport coats, where she stuffed the journal inside her Sesame Street Underoos and remained an hour, until she heard her mother calling.

In his attic bedroom, on the bed, hugging his knees, back against wood paneling, shivering from the cold sweat filming his body, "Waiting for the Worms" from *The Wall* playing on the Radio Shack *Realistic* tape recorder—

"Make it stop," Griff whispered, feeling his lips move, but unsure if he'd actually said anything.

At the top of the stairs, a furry, obese creature appeared.

"Please don't hurt me," Griff pleaded.

"Meow," the creature said.

"Can you make it stop?"

"Meow."

Stacy's first drawing in the new journal was done in black ink, a scowling, hunched over old lady whose body was surrounded by short, squiggly lines.

She admired it for a minute, then, from the Crayola box, selected *Brick Red*, and drew an "X" on the page.

"Ah-ah-ah," she laughed.

"Os-car!" and "F-D-N-Y!" they chanted at the WHFD station, the trucks parked outside to make room in the garage for the celebration, where a CONGRATULATIONS OSCAR! banner signed by the guys had been strung to the wall, and a keg of Budweiser had been tapped, sent over by Community Tavern along with several bottles of Welch's white grape juice.

"I'm proud of you, kid," said Captain Rawley, arm around Oscar. "What did your pop say when you told him?"

"I haven't yet."

The table at the Grove Street townhouse in the West Village had been impeccably set for the dinner party of four couples, one of whom was Bruce, in chaps, leather vest, and leather biker cap, and Philip, dressed as Little Bo Peep.

The food and wine were good and the talk was lively. At one point Philip leaned over and said into Bruce's ear, "I'm sorry for snapping at you earlier, Bruce, but you were right. I am having a good time."

"Just wait until dessert, Philip. I know exactly what you want, and it's okay with me. I know what I want too." He looked at Betty Page seated across the table and winked.

"Time for dessert!" said the mustached man in NYPD uniform and mirrored sunglasses at the head of the table, utility belt sagging suggestively from waist. "Bo Peep, would you mind giving me a hand in the kitchen?"

"Go have fun, Philip," Bruce said.

On the living room couch of her home in Hempstead Gardens, Leona Crane, in her new olive green textured cover journal, wrote in impeccable cursive:

Today's children have no respect. While shopping for this very journal, I saw a similar one with a beautiful crimson cover that, after searching tirelessly in the bin, I had the good fortune to find, only to have it snatched from my grasp by a horrible little girl

Her narrative was interrupted by the doorbell.

"Who would be calling at this hour?" she asked aloud, then called, "Coming!"

She opened the door and, through the storm door window, saw a black man and woman standing on the stoop, both about her own age, the man in a suit, the woman a pink dress like one would wear to church.

"What do you want?" Leona screamed through the door.

"Good evening, madam," the man said. "We are servants of God here to tell you about Jehovah—"

"Madam? Just who are you calling 'madam'? And just what in the hell are you doing in our neighborhood? I should call Detective Smith and have you arrested for trespassing!"

"Let's go," the woman said to the man, and both turned to leave.

"Stay out of our neighborhood!" shouted Leona Crane, just before slamming the door.

"How dare these people come into our neighborhood and disturb me in my home," she grumbled, shuffling back to the couch, heart racing, lightheaded.

Just as she was about to sit back down, her body became

immobile, eyes fixed on the olive green journal, the last thing she would see in her 81 years.

The parking lot was full, the new Shopper's Village weekend flea market now open in the space where Korvette's had been.

Griff, with a dollar and some change stolen from his mother's purse, who, minutes earlier, had been told by her to stay away from this specific place, crossed busy Westminster Road, where he picked up a woman's voice echoing across the lot with burlesque inflection belonging to a tall, beautiful black woman in front of the entrance, next to her a display of ladies' handbags—

"Fashion handbags, ladies, only six dollars for these beautiful handbags, only six dollars, ladies, booth 129, ladies, fashion handbags, ladies, only six dollars..."

Most of the people going in were black. The large, bright, open space of departments and bins and white people had been replaced by a soft lit city grid of vendor booths, many selling things he'd never seen at Korvette's or TSS or Shop Rite or any of the other stores his mother dragged he and his sister to. In front of The Pickle Man's booth, there was a huge wooden barrel of dills floating in brine that could be smelled everywhere on the first floor. Many booths were selling t-shirts, caps, sneakers, jeans, sunglasses. Some were selling food items like the big soft pretzels they sold on street corners in Manhattan, and sweets like candy, baked goods, and ice cream. Others were selling electronics, records, tapes, collectibles, handmade crafts, makeup, hair products, wigs, perfume, comic books, baseball cards, Smurf figurines, *Star Wars* action figures, Atari cartridges.

He walked the entire grid until arriving at a dead end in the far back corner of the building, where there were two booths, *Madame Me'shelle's Fortune Telling* and, across the aisle, *Clifford's Comics & Rags*.

"You Jerry?" Fred asked the large, bearded man with the sunglasses and black pocket t-shirt, backstage at the Nassau Veterans Memorial Coliseum, where the Grateful Dead were getting ready to play the second show of a three-night stand.

"Yeah, I am," he said, lighting a Marlboro. "Hey, are you Light Bulb Guy?"

"Yeah," Fred said, lighting a Winston. "You wanted to see me?"

"Oh, wow, you've got Winstons... I haven't had one of those in ages. Mind if I bum one?"

Fred shook one out of the pack and Jerry tossed his Marlboro.

"Thanks, man."

"What did you want to see me about?"

"I noticed last night when we were playing 'Althea' that the house lighting was amazing, and there were signs everywhere for Slate Bulb & Electric, so I asked around and found out that you were the man."

"That's right. I'm the man."

"Anyway, we also use our own stage lighting, and it's seen better days—a lot of the equipment got damaged when we went to Egypt and got sand all over everything. Long story short, we need some new lights, man."

"I can help. I helped Pink Floyd when they came through here a few months ago. Them and that stupid wall. Giant cardboard bricks everywhere. Big fucking mess, except for the lights. Here's my card."

After school, at the Burger King on Hempstead Turnpike next to the miniature golf course and George Washington Elementary, in his booth in the back near the bathrooms and out of view from the front counter, Griff watched the approach of his next customer, Mike Molloy, who slid into the seat across from him.

"Got any *Hustler*?" Mike asked.

"Only July."

"I already have that one."

"*Playboy*? *Penthouse*? *Swing Shift*?"

"What *Penthouse* do you have?"

"March, April, June."

"How much for April and June?"

"Four."

Mike reached into his jeans pocket and produced four crumpled singles, while Griff pulled the requested issues from his knapsack.

The cold open was a bold decision, as was everything else about the pilot episode of *Magnum P.I.*, premiering on CBS, December 11, 1980, a man with a Chevron mustache swimming in a tidal pool that looked much like the one at the Ahu Akbaba Resort—

"What the hell is this?" Roger asked aloud, leaning

forward in his recliner, reaching for the Viceroy 100s.

"It's funny, the things a grown man will do for a living," said a voice in the television, but the action on the screen wasn't showing anyone speaking.

"Who said that?" Roger asked aloud, lighting his cigarette.

"Especially me," the voice continued. *"Take this morning. I'm trying to break into Robin Masters's estate—you know, the writer, the one with all the best sellers, all that money—"*

"It's like I can hear his thoughts," Roger said.

"Roger, who are you talking to in there?" Joyce asked from the living room.

"Nobody. I'm just thinking out loud."

Next they cut to Old Pickle Puss from *The Betty White Show* dressed in khaki shirt and shorts like he's on a safari, handling two angry Dobermans that he unleashes on the mustached man. Then there's a flashback scene from the war of the swimming man and his two buddies—

"Holy cow!" Roger exclaimed.

"What are you watching?" Joyce asked, entering the room.

"Magnum P.I."

"Never heard of it."

"It's new."

Joyce watched for a moment, arms folded.

"That one guy kind of looks like you when you were in the Army," she said.

"No he doesn't."

"I think he does a little. And those other two guys look like your Army friends who were at our wedding."

"They do not!"

"Jeez, Rog, no need to get defensive."

"Here I am, just sitting here trying to watch TV, and you come in here accusing me of being in a top-secret military spy program!"

"I did not!"

"Now who's getting defensive?"

Griff, knapsack full and straining the old Army green straps, crossed Westminster Road, and was walking in front of the Flower Time nursery towards Oak Street when a siren wailed in his ear.

He turned to see a flashing red light atop the unmarked cruiser beside him.

"Hey, Griffin!" his grandfather said, leaning over to the open passenger side window.

"Hi, Grandpa."

"Where you going with that knapsack on a Saturday?"

"Home."

"Where are you coming from?"

"Woolworth's."

"Woolworth's? You didn't go into that flea market, did you?"

"No."

"That knapsack looks pretty heavy."

"My textbooks are heavy."

"Textbooks? What are you studying these days? Mind if I take a look?"

"What's that red spot on your neck, Grandpa?"

"On my neck?" he asked, rubbing his neck.

"There's a dark red spot on your neck."

"Oh, that. It's just a little rash."

"There's another one on the other side."

"Well, that's the way these things are, Griffin. You know

what, pal? Grandpa's gotta run, but you keep hitting those books, okay, champ?"

"Okay, Grandpa."

Joyce heard shouts outside and looked out the front window to see a black man in a Shopper's Village security guard uniform tackle a black man on the front lawn. They wrestled briefly, but the man who'd been tackled broke free and continued up the driveway into the backyard with the guard in hot pursuit, and over the chain link fence into the yard behind them and down their driveway.

"Did you see that?" Joyce asked Roger, who was in the den watching an old *Abbott and Costello* film.

"See what?" he asked.

"Another security guard chasing a shoplifter from that goddamn flea market, and this time the security guard tackled him in our front yard! Look what they did to the lawn! There's a huge chunk missing!"

"There is?"

"You didn't hear them yelling?"

"I heard something, but I didn't know what it was."

"And you weren't curious enough to get up and see what it was? You know, in case someone was murdering the kids or something?"

"I was watching *Abbott and Costello*."

"So, Roger, if one of them busts in and rapes me and I'm crying for help, are you just going to sit there watching *Abbott and Costello*?"

"No. I would help if that happened."

"God, Roger, could you possibly be any more useless?"

"Useless? I work hard all week to support this family, and you come in here and call me 'useless' when I'm trying to relax?"

"I'm sorry, Roger. You're not totally useless. Just when you're at home."

"So, it's my fault that security guards are chasing shoplifters through our front yard?"

"No, Roger! But we have to move! Look what's happening to our neighborhood! We never saw anything like this when Korvette's was there!"

"Philip, I really think it's time to see a doctor."

"I'm fine, Bruce. It's just a few little rashes."

"It's more than a few rashes, Philip, and they're not going away. They're all over your body. And you've lost so much weight. Please, Philip, for me, go see a doctor."

"Alright, Bruce. I'll call in the morning."

"That old Bug your trade-in?" asked Eugene, senior salesman at Green Acres Datsun in Valley Stream, near the mall.

"Yep," Roger said, looking at the old beige Beetle he'd inherited from Joyce after she got the Granada.

"Well, I'll be able to knock off a couple of bucks, but I'm really the one doing you the favor by taking that piece of crap off your hands."

"That's fine."

"I'm glad you see it that way, Mr. Ramsey. I like your

attitude, and your style, though it does seem a little cold for shorts and sandals. I dig that shirt, though, and those are some great sunglasses. Let me guess—you're a *Magnum P.I.* guy."

"Uh, yeah. I like *Magnum P.I.*"

"Of course. What red-blooded American man doesn't? I've seen plenty of guys just like you, Mr. Ramsey, come through these very doors looking to add a little cool to their wardrobe, who don't want to mortgage the house on a Ferrari."

"You've seen others like me?"

"Sure, Mr. Ramsey, sure. They're coming in all the time, right off the streets. Look, there goes one now."

"Where?"

"Uh, you just missed him. Anyway, as I was saying, Roger—may I call you Roger? You already feel like family."

"Sure. Can I call you 'Eugene'?"

"Of course, Rog, of course. Anyway, as I was saying, Rog, Ferrari in Italian means *'expensive headache'*. The Italians build cars for performance, not endurance. The Japanese, however, build cars that are not only cool, like the San Marzano Red B310 with power windows, A/C, CB, AM/FM, and Optional Rally Fun Pack, which is the one all the Magnum-heads have been going with, but they'll run forever. I can assure you, Rog—or should I call you *Ramsey, P.I.?*—that, if you're going *Magnum* on a budget, this is your automobile."

At Mercy Hospital, Griff and Stacy followed Joyce into the room where their grandfather was unconscious on a bed, tubes stuck into nostrils and arms, face gaunt, muscle hanging from bone, dark splotches covering otherwise ashen skin.

"You kids go cheer Grandpa up," Joyce said, then turned

to Bruce and asked if she could have a word with him outside.

Bruce followed her out of the room and to the end of the hall, next to a staircase door and a window overlooking the Southern State Parkway.

"You did this to him!" she said angrily, under her breath. "You made him sick!"

"Then how am I not sick?"

"I don't know, but I saw something on *60 Minutes* about this virus that affects gay men, and this is your fault!"

"Your father is a gay man."

Joyce slapped him across the face.

"My father is not gay! You're the pervert, and you tricked him into doing all this gay shit and he did it because you're his friend and he trusted you, and now he's dying! This is on you, Bruce!"

"I gotta hand it to you guys," said John Backe, in his office at Black Rock, to Donald P. Bellisario and Glen A. Larson, handing each a Partagás. "I thought it was a bold idea from the start, but who would of thought we'd have such a hit on our hands! And now Stallone is doing a film about a Vietnam veteran. Good times, gentlemen, good times!"

The stretch of Hempstead Turnpike in West Hempstead had been closed by the Nassau County Police Department for the funeral procession, the hearse transporting the body of Detective Philip Smith leading a seemingly endless line of police cruisers shimmering in the cold morning sunlight, from not only Nassau, but from Suffolk, the independent villages and hamlets, NYPD, New York State Troopers, Westchester, Albany, Philadelphia, Washington DC, small towns all over the state, and various departments from New Jersey, Connecticut, Pennsylvania, Massachusetts, and Delaware.

A small set of risers had been set up in the Burger King parking lot, where Joyce was seated next to Oscar, in FDNY Class A uniform, and, on the other side of him, his fiancé, Theresa. Roger, in his Customs Blues, was on Joyce's other side, and the kids on the other side of him. In the rows below, members of NCPD's top brass in their Class A's. On the restaurant roof, seven marksmen standing at attention.

The procession stopped. Everyone on the risers rose. A bugler played "Taps". Three rounds were fired by the marksmen.

Oscar, Theresa, Joyce, Roger, and the kids were shown to a limousine that followed the hearse to the cemetery.

The capacity crowd at the Nassau Veterans Memorial Coliseum counted down the last seconds of the third period, then erupted with a roar that nearly blew the roof off the barn, as the New York Islanders won their second consecutive Stanley Cup with a 4-1 series victory over the Minnesota North Stars.

The entire building was shaking, but, perhaps nowhere more than up in the Slate Bulb & Electric Company luxury suite, where the floor was bowing visibly under the weight of Dolly jumping up and down in her home-white autographed #22 Mike Bossy jersey, her big orange hair being flattened by the ceiling tiles. At the front of the suite, where Fred had watched the final period with Mike Ramone, whose company, Hammersmith Nuclear, had the suite next door, the shaking caused Fred to drop his Scotch tumbler to the crowd below, and he nearly fell out himself until Mike secured him.

"Thanks, Mike," Fred said a few minutes later, after the crowd had settled down and preparations were being made on the ice for the Cup ceremony. "Listen, we're gonna have a party for the team at my house in a few days if you wanna stop by. We had one last year and it was a blast. They even brought the Cup."

"You live up on the North Shore, right?"

"That's right."

"Like Gatsby."

"Yeah, but I'm not a loser like him."

On their yacht cruising the Long Island Sound, upon which she and her husband were hosting a cocktail party for their Greenwich friends, Belinda Pennington raised her bloody Mary and announced, "I want to make a toast."

"Another one, dear?" asked her husband, Chuck.

"Last one, I promise. But let me stand up here, this is a good one."

"Please be careful, dear, remember last time—"

"Oh, hush, Chuck."

In her heels, bloody Mary in hand, she climbed atop one of the bench seats covered with white leather cushions and attempted to find her balance, until the boat crossed the wake of another vessel, causing a bump. In the blink of an eye she was gone, the only sound in the absence of her voice that of the humming engine.

"Swenson, dear boy!" Chuck called to the wheelhouse. "Can you turn the boat around, please? My wife has fallen overboard again."

"Yes, sir," Swenson called back.

On the pool deck of the Flynt Estate on the North Shore, Joyce, legs outstretched on a deck chair, margarita on the small table beside her, lit a cigarette, and stared across the night lit water at Bobby Rydell and his band performing "Volare".

She then looked over at the kitchen window screen, through which she saw Roger, drunk, in his Hawaiian shirt and baseball cap, holding a giant beer stein, loudly asking Islander head coach Al Arbour if Canadian Customs had ever searched his suitcase. Next to them, Fred was telling team president Bill Torrey about how all of the public golf courses on Long Island were covered with geese shit. She then looked back across the pool at Bobby, who smiled at her as he sang.

The sliding screen door opened and out of the house stepped a mustached man with dark, curly hair, who looked a little like Burt Reynolds, but shorter.

He slid the door closed and came straight to her.

"Howdy," he said, standing over her, lighting a Marlboro. "Having fun?"

"Not really," she said. "Do I know you? You look familiar."

"No. I would have remembered a beauty like you. Mike Ramone."

"Joyce Ramsey," she said, reaching for her margarita and attempting to sip it, but the salted rim missed her lips and some of the drink spilled onto her Sassons. "Shit. Shoot. I'm sorry, I've been here too long. I'm also married."

"You're Roger's wife."

"You know Roger?"

"No."

"Then how do you know I'm Roger's wife?"

"Someone told me."

"Who?"

"Fred."

"Oh."

"Oh?"

"I'm Dolly's friend. Not really a big Fred fan."

He laughed.

"Mind if I sit next to you?"

"Be my guest."

He sat and spread his legs out.

"Any requests?" Bobby called from across the pool.

"I'll Never Dance Again," Joyce called back. Bobby gave her a thumbs up.

"Big Rydell fan?" Mike asked.

"I feel kind of bad for him. He had a bit of a comeback with *Grease*, but now here he is right back in Dolly's backyard."

Inside the house, the noise level escalated when goaltender Billy "Hatchet Man" Smith went downstairs to Fred's rec room and started trashing it with one of his own autographed goalie sticks. Many of his teammates hurried downstairs to spectate, only to find him gently replacing the stick back on the wall where he'd found it.

In the vacated kitchen, Dolly had superstar right winger Mike Bossy trapped against the counter. From behind a closed door in a distant wing of the house, the echo of a woman could be heard pleading, "Denny, please don't hit me!" and a man yelling at her to "Shut up!"

"Have you been to a Flynt party before?" Joyce asked.

"This is my first. Fred's luxury suite at the Coliseum is next to my company's, and sometimes I go over there because they're usually having more fun."

"What company do you work for?"

"Hammersmith Nuclear. I sell parts and equipment to nuclear power plants all over the world."

"Oh," she said, exhaling, "that sounds exotic."

"Not as exotic as the woman before my eyes."

"Oh, God."

"You seem thrilled to be here."

"I didn't want to come, but Roger got into the whole hockey thing and wanted to hang out with the players. Why aren't you in there with them?"

"I was in there, but I was bored. Then I saw something interesting out here. And it wasn't Bobby Rydell."

"Oh, God—"

There was another commotion inside when "Mr. Islander", right winger Bobby Nystrom, who'd been in the foyer ladling Molson Golden from the Stanley Cup into drinking glasses, burst into the kitchen exclaiming, "The Rangers are here! The Rangers are here!"

Islander players swarmed the foyer, which had been infiltrated by members of the rival New York Rangers, among them co-captains Barry Beck and Dave Maloney, centerman Ron Duguay, left winger Don Maloney, defenseman Ron Greschner, and goaltender John "JD" Davidson. Fights broke out all over the room, men pulling each other's shirts off, throwing punches, head-butting, a Ming vase shattering over someone's head, beer sloshing out of the Cup.

On the pool deck, where Bobby and the band had

abandoned their instruments to watch the action in the foyer—

"It sounds like Fred's luxury suite in there," Mike said to Joyce.

"We usually leave when the fights break out," Joyce said, getting up from the deck chair. "It was nice meeting you, Mike."

Behind the wheel of the B310, Roger, in red Hawaiian shirt, khaki shorts, Detroit Tigers away cap with orange "D", aviator sunglasses, and Puma *Easy Riders* sans socks, pulled into a vacant parking spot on Sound Beach Avenue in Old Greenwich, in front of the office of Billy Odenkirk, Attorney at Law, then went inside.

"Pleasure to meet you, Mr. Ramsey," the attorney said, extending his hand, "and I'm very sorry for your loss. Please have a seat."

Roger lit a cigarette and sat in one of the chairs facing the large walnut desk. Odenkirk slid a crystal ashtray to him.

"As you know, Mr. Ramsey, you are half owner of your parents' old house in Franklin Square—"

"I am?"

"Of course. Who do you think owned it?"

"I kind of forgot about it. But Belinda, I guess."

"She did own the other half of it, and there was no mortgage. When your mother passed, the two of you became the owners together, but your share was held in a trust until you turned twenty-five. Your sister and her husband have been my clients for many years, and I didn't even realize she owned this. It is very possible that she simply forgot about it.

Her husband is quite financially secure, so it may have gotten buried in their portfolio of properties. Anyhow, Mr. Ramsey, with her unfortunate passing, and, with the blessing of the widower, Mr. Pennington, who also wasn't aware of this property and didn't want anything to do with it, the house now belongs solely to you."

In the lobby of One World Trade Center—

"All clear," Oscar said into his radio mouthpiece, after he and Walsh finished inspecting the faulty floor socket that had caused the minor electrical fire, now extinguished.

"This place is pretty amazing," Walsh said, looking up at the large tridents housing the windows and the ceiling lights high above.

"Yeah," Oscar said, also looking up. "Ever been up top?"

"Nah. You?"

"Not yet. I'll get up there one of these days."

Behind the wheel of the B310 racing down Rockaway Boulevard—

"I've been a Customs man for over a decade, and this is the first time I've ever been sent home early," Roger said aloud, having been sent home early after an electrical fire at International Arrivals closed the TWA terminal. *"It's not often that a hardworking family man like me suddenly finds himself with nearly an entire day to do whatever he wants, and I'm not about to let it go to waste. But first, a little breakfast."*

Making no mention of the breakfast Joyce had made him less than three hours earlier—stack of Bisquick pancakes, bacon, scrambled eggs, toast—he pulled into the parking lot of the Airport Diner. Inside, he was seated at a booth overlooking the Boulevard and asked the waitress to bring him a cheese Danish and coffee while he looked at the menu. He decided on "The Hercules"—buttermilk pancakes stacked high, a plate-sized Belgian waffle, three eggs sunny-side up, a plate of bacon, ham, hash browns, toast stacked high, tall orange juice, and bottomless cup of coffee.

After his plates had been scraped clean, he drank coffee and smoked cigarettes while flipping through the *Newsday* sports section for the second time, and ordered another Danish.

An hour later, back behind the wheel of the B310—

"I'm not ready to head back to the estate just yet, so I'm going to take the backroads home. There's nowhere other than the toilet where a man can think more clearly than driving through the backroads in a hot set of wheels."

Half-hour later he was back in West Hempstead. He turned onto Oak Street, where he encountered a black Trans Am parked in his driveway spot behind Joyce's Granada.

"I know what you're thinking, and you're right. It's not every day a man comes home and finds a strange Trans Am in his driveway, so I know something's up."

He drove past the house and around the block until he was back on Oak Street, parking several houses from his own.

Holding the gym bag that had been on the passenger side floor of the B310, he looked around, then proceeded on the sidewalk towards his own house. He went up the driveway and into the garage, where he changed into his Hawaiian shirt, khaki shorts, Tigers home cap with the white "D", aviator sunglasses, and *Easy Riders*, no socks. He cocked his Customs-issue Glock and stuffed it into the back of his shorts, then proceeded to the back door of the house, using his key to unlock it, but pretending he was picking it.

There were sex noises in the living room. He drew his gun and proceeded through the kitchen and down the hall, stopping before the living room.

He closed his eyes, took a breath, then made his move.

"Freeze!" he yelled, pointing the Glock at the nude mustached man atop his nude wife on the couch.

The man looked up and smiled.

"Howdy!" he said.

Griff, in his attic bedroom organizing inventory, Michael Jackson's *Thriller* playing on his new double-cassette deck boom box, heard his mother call from downstairs that dinner was ready.

He finished up and packed everything away, then headed down to the kitchen, stopping cold when he saw his mother and smirking sister already seated, and the vacant space at the head of the table.

"Where's Roger?" he asked.

On Dogwood Avenue in Franklin Square, Roger pulled the B310 next to the curb and cut the engine.

He got out and crossed the sidewalk, then grasped with both hands the sagging chain link fence surrounding the condemned property. Inside the fence, the yard was overgrown and the windows on the house had been boarded with plywood.

Minutes later, behind the wheel of the B310—

"There's a time in every man's life when he realizes he can't go home again," he said aloud, *"and there's really only one thing he can do in moments like these."*

He pulled into the Dan's Supreme parking lot, then went into the store and emerged with two six packs of Bud longnecks and a carton of Viceroy 100s. He walked by the B310, crossed Dogwood, and proceeded to the old corner, where he twisted the cap off one of the longnecks and pulled a pack from the carton.

In the living room, Joyce and Mike, wearing matching tight white tennis outfits with sweaters tied around their necks, sharing a pack of Kent Golden Lights 100s, holding hands across two chairs, facing Griff and Stacy on the couch—

"Mike is a very special friend of mine," Joyce said to the kids, "and he's going to be around a lot more—a *lot* more—so I wanted you guys to meet him and to get to know him, which is why we'll be spending the day at his company's picnic. Mike is the Executive Vice President of Sales at Hammersmith Nuclear, which sells parts to nuclear power plants all over the world."

"Howdy!" Mike exclaimed.

Griff and Stacy stared.

"Aren't you guys going to say 'howdy' to Mike?"

"No," Griff said.

Stacy shook her head.

Roger and Nancy, the gold-blazered real estate agent, standing outside the sagging chain link fence surrounding the condemned Franklin Square property—

"Mr. Ramsey," Nancy said, "you'll get a lot more for the house if you just make the necessary repairs."

"I need to sell now. Today, if possible. First cash offer."

"Ah-ah-ah," Stacy laughed after finishing her latest sketch in the crimson journal, this one of the mustached man in the tight white tennis outfit and bulbous crotch, on the page following the one she'd drawn of her obese father, wearing a flowery Hawaiian shirt, baseball cap, and short shorts, leaning on a Datsun.

She turned back to the previous page and looked at her father, then turned back to the man in the tennis outfit, then back again.

Shrugging, she reached for the Brick Red and X'd out her father, then closed the journal.

At the top of the Empire State Building—

Joyce and a group of tourists from St. Louis gasped when Mike, on a knee in front of her, opened the ring box.

"Oh my God, Mike! I've never seen a diamond that big!"

"Joyce, when your divorce is finalized, will you marry me?"

"Yes! Of course!"

She kissed Mike and the tourists applauded politely.

At King Dick's Lūʻau Lounge in south central Waikiki—

"It looks like you swallowed the Goodyear blimp," Dick said, hugging Roger. "You should have told me you were coming, big guy, I would have set something up. What are you doing here, anyway?"

"I just moved here."

"What? With Joyce and the kids?"

"No, just me."

"What about Joyce?"

"She's a whore."

"Ah. You got jellyfished and ran away to paradise. Good move, slim. What about the kids?"

"Right. The kids. They'll be fine with Joyce."

"And what are you gonna do out here? Did Customs give you a transfer?"

"I quit. I'm gonna be a P.I."

"You're still stuck on that old bit? C.T. was just kidding about that, you know. And you do know that you need a license to be a private dick."

"You do?"

"Of course, Sherlock. You should have just put in for a transfer to Honolulu International instead of quitting and giving up your pension and health insurance."

"Crap, I didn't think of that."

"Well, don't sweat it, pal. I'll talk to my buddy, Toothpick. He can probably help you out with that license and throw you a case or two to get started. Right now, though, I gotta get ready for ladies' night, so let me run you over to C.T.'s place in the Benz, he's just up the road. Maybe he can take you up for a quick flight. Who would have thought that stupid chopper tour business idea would actually fly, right?"

In the backyard of a half-acre waterfront property on the Great South Bay in Massapequa's Biltmore Shores, Mike and Joyce both lit Kent Golden Lights 100s, then Mike turned to his third-cousin, Jimmy, and asked, "Don't you think seven hundred thousand is a little much?"

"Uncle Tommy still has some outstanding debt and refuses to lower the price," Jimmy said. "That's why nobody will even come and look at the house at this point. That, and also what happened to Uncle Tony and Aunt Genie downstairs. Say, can I get one of those long cigarettes?"

"What happened?" Joyce asked.

"Heart attacks," Mike said. "They both died of heart attacks down there."

"At the same time?"

"Yep. When Aunt Genie found Uncle Tony and saw that he was having a heart attack, she went into cardiac arrest."

"Jeez."

"Yeah, Jeez," Jimmy said.

"Can you give us a minute, Jimmy?" Mike asked.

"Sure thing, Mikey."

Mike and Joyce walked over to the Chris Craft Catalina dry-docked on the backyard lawn.

"What do you think?" Mike asked.

"It's beautiful. A lot of marble for my taste, but I always wanted to live on the water. And I don't imagine there would be any shoplifters running through the yard here."

Inside the office of Island Skippers Helicopter Tours—

"Well, Rog, this is your lucky day," C.T. said. "I have to run some medical supplies to a children's hospital over on Moloka'i and you can ride shotgun. But first I have to ask you something, and don't take it personal, I just gotta make sure with the cargo we don't get too heavy—how much you weigh these days?"

"Two ninety," Roger said.

"Two ninety? For real, Rog?"

"Give or take a few pounds. Maybe three hundred. Three ten. Three fifteen."

"And when was the last time you stepped on a scale?"

"Last week."

"Alright, Rog, I'll take your word for it."

Liftoff in the brown, orange, and yellow chopper was wobbly, but C.T. was able to smooth out over Māmala Bay, until a red light started flashing on the panel, followed by a buzzing alarm.

"Roger, be honest with me, your life depends on it—how much you really weigh?"

"Four twenty five."

"Four twenty five? Motherfucker! I knew you weren't two-ninety, but I had no idea you were *that* much!"

"Sorry."

"You ain't the only one, motherfucker. Alright, here's what we're gonna do. You're gonna reach under the seat and grab a life vest, and I'm going to lower down as close as I can to the water, and you're gonna jump out. I'll radio for a rescue boat to come get you, so all you gotta do is float for a few minutes until it gets there. Understood?"

Roger didn't answer.

"I ain't messin' around, Rog. This chopper's gonna crash if you don't get out, and those sick kids won't get these medical supplies. I'll push you out if I have to. Now reach under the seat and grab a life vest."

Roger pulled two vests from beneath the seat. Unable to buckle one of the vests around his girth, he slung an arm through each of them.

C.T. lowered the chopper, hovering five feet above the water.

"Don't worry, Rog, you'll be fine. Just float there for a few minutes and the boat will come get you."

Door open, sitting sideways, looking down at the water, Roger jumped on "three". On the way down, his feet hit the landing skid, causing the chopper to wobble, and causing him to hit himself in the face with his forearm and break his nose before slap-landing on the Pacific.

C.T. stabilized the chopper and flew away. Roger, afloat, nose bleeding, looked around and saw no boats and heard no engines other than the one belonging to the chopper disappearing into the distance.

Bobbing, he watched the clouds and checked his bloody nose with the back of his hand.

There was a splash nearby. He rolled his head to the left and saw a fin. It disappeared, then reappeared and went by again. He rolled his head the other way and saw the fin again.

"Maybe he'll leave me alone if I'm nice to him," he said aloud, then, addressing the circling fin, "Hello, Mr. Shark. My name is Roger. What's your name?"

At the White Castle in Lynbrook—

"Kids," Joyce said, seated in the booth across from her two children, a tray of heavily onioned little hamburgers between them, freshly lit Kent Golden Light 100 burning between her fingers, "there's a reason I took you here for dinner tonight."

"I don't like onions," Griff said. "Can we go to Burger King?"

"The reason," she continued, exhaling, starting to cry, "is that your father and I used to come here."

"Aren't these burgers too small for him?"

"He liked them. He just ate a lot of them. Anyway, the reason we're here is that I have something very sad to tell you, and I thought it might be helpful to tell you in a place he loved..."

She started to sob.

"Is Daddy dead?" Griff asked, scraping the onions off one of the burgers with a napkin.

"I'm afraid so," Joyce cried. "There was an accident in Hawaii. I don't know exactly what happened, but he was in a helicopter with one of his Army friends and somehow fell out and got eaten by a shark, which was then eaten by a killer whale."

Griff stopped scraping and looked at his crying mother, then at his sister. His lips began to quiver and his body began to spasm, then he started to laugh.

"Ah-ah-ah," Stacy laughed.

Joyce, cheeks stained with mascara tears, watched her children laugh, and was soon laughing with them.

"Let's go to Burger King," she said when they finally caught their breath.

Still giggling, they slid out of the booth, leaving the tray of heavily onioned little hamburgers on the table.

At the Budweiser brewery in St. Louis, Missouri —

August Anheuser Busch III, affectionately known as "Three Sticks", President and CEO of the Anheuser-Busch Companies, looked out at the hundreds of employees assembled between the great vats filled with *The World Famous Budweiser Beer*, hard hats covering hearts, heads bowed, machines shut down, the only sounds the buzzing fluorescent lights overhead and the voice of their leader echoing through the great hall.

"Let us take a moment," he said, "to pause and reflect upon the life of one of this company's greatest ever individual customers, a man named Roger Ramsey, U.S. Army veteran and true American hero, whom we recently lost to the Pacific just off the coast of Hawaii."

Not a sound was made until Mr. Busch somberly thanked them and the machines were switched back on.

At CBS Black Rock —

"Let me get this straight," said John Backe to the writers seated in front of his desk, Glen A. Larson in black suit and black shirt with red tie, and Donald P. Bellisario in flowery blue Hawaiian shirt and Los Angeles Dodgers cap, "an entire episode where Magnum is treading water in the ocean with a shark swimming around him? That sounds boring. This is

CBS, gentlemen, not PBS."

"He'll be thinking out loud," Bellisario said.

"And talking to the shark," Larson added.

"Talking to the shark? Does the shark talk back?"

"No, but Magnum starts having flashbacks. Intense childhood memories of his father timing him in the water."

"And then he's rescued in the nick of time."

"And then the shark swims away."

Backe leaned back in his chair, put his feet on the desk, and lit his Partagás.

"I have one word, gentleman," he said. "Bold."

In the *Clifford's Comics & Rags* booth at Shopper's Village—

"Moving?" Clifford asked. "And you gotta go with them?"

"I don't have any choice," Griff said. "Mama sold our digs and she and the Bandit bought some fancy crib out in the sticks."

"Where?"

"Massapequa."

"Massapequa? Damn, G, that's way out near Suffolk County. This sucks. I was making good money off you hustling those back issues. What are you gonna do out there?"

"I don't know."

"I'll tell you what. I know a guy out in Amityville, 'Big Bart'. Amityville is across the border in Suffolk, but it's close to Massapequa. He got all kinds of shit goin' on, and he can hook you up with something. Here's his card. I'll let him know you're a hustler and to be expecting you."

He handed Griff a business card that said "Bart Mart" in big red letters with an address below it on Route 110 in

Amityville.

"Thanks, C."

"Damn, G. I'm about to cry. You better come back and visit, alright?"

"I will."

In the executive offices at Shea Stadium in Flushing, Queens—

"I know the standings don't show it yet," said Fred Wilpon, President and CEO of the New York Mets, to Fred Flynt, "but we've got a lot of fine young talent and a savvy veteran in Keith Hernandez to lead them."

"Is he gonna stay? I heard he was crying when he got traded here."

"Yes, well, Rusty took him under his wing and showed him the city, and now he's seen the talent that's here and in the pipeline, so now he wants to stay. Fred, this'll be like the Islanders back in the day, only we have greater exposure than the NHL. This is America's pastime, Major League Baseball. Slate Bulb & Electric placards will be up there with the Marlboro man, Budweiser, RC Cola, Charles Chips, Manufacturers Hanover, and *Newsday*, and you'll have national exposure on the NBC *Game of the Week*."

"Alright," said Fred Flynt, extending his hand, "I'm in."

At Rick's Skyway Bar inside the TWA terminal at LAX—

Red-eyed and silent after a week in Waikiki, where Joyce and Mike were wed during a sunset ceremony on the beach overlooking Māmala Bay and had spent the rest of the honeymoon in their suite having sex, their connecting flight back to JFK was now delayed three hours, the newlyweds seated at the bar staring into their bloody Marys, letting the Kent Golden Lights 100s in the ashtray burn.

"Oh my God, it's, like, The Hammer!" a woman nearby exclaimed.

They turned to see two large-breasted, tube-topped, overtanned blondes coming towards them, who took the vacant spot at the bar on Mike's free side.

"You're, like, the Hammer," one of them said.

"Can we, like, get your autograph or something?" the other asked.

Blushing, Mike looked at Joyce and shrugged, then turned back to the two women.

"I think you've got me confused with someone else," he said.

"So, you're, like, not, like, The Hammer?"

"Nope."

The one closest him looked at his wedding band and at Joyce's engagement ring, then turned back to her friend.

"I think, like, The Hammer is married to this old lady."

"Gag me with a spoon."

"Yeah, grody to the max. Come on, let's, like, go drink somewhere else."

They laughed all the way out of the bar.

"What the hell was that?" Joyce asked.

"I guess they just think everybody's a movie star out here," he said, sipping his bloody Mary.

At the crib in Biltmore Shores —

"Can we watch *The Godfather* again, Uncle Jimmy?" Griff asked. "And get pizza with triple extra cheese? And can I have another one of your beers?"

"I think it's your sister's turn to pick the movie," Jimmy said. "What do you wanna watch, sweetheart?"

Stacy looked at the stack of VHS tapes they had rented from South Shore Video and pointed to *The Exorcist*.

"Again with *The Exorcist*?"

Stacy nodded.

"Alright, alright. You's is good kids. I'm gonna miss yas when your ma and Mikey get back. I'll order the pizza. Hey, Griff, you ever have quadruple extra cheese?"

"*Quadruple* extra cheese? No fuckin' way! They have that here?"

"Sure. You see, kid, Massapequa ain't so bad. The bagels are pretty good too. That's why they call this place Matzah-Pizza."

The package, wrapped in brown grocery bag paper, arrived a few days before Christmas. The address label was typed with her newly taken name, Joyce Ramone, and the postmark was from Plandome, NY.

Inside was a VHS cassette, the label torn off, stopped halfway through.

Mike was at work and the kids were at school.

She brought the tape into the living room and ejected the

one in the VCR, *Best Friends*, starring Burt Reynolds and Goldie Hawn, then inserted the new one.

She pressed "PLAY" and turned on the television, then gasped and pressed "STOP".

It was a long pedal on the Huffy, a mile from the crib up to Merrick road, and another mile up to Sunrise Highway, then around the bend past Sunrise Mall and White Castle to County Line Road, beyond which the smooth asphalt shoulder turned to broken gravel in the shadow of the South Oaks Psychiatric Hospital. From there it was north on Route 110, most of the stores boarded up except the fast food joints and the DMV, to a weathered bodega in the shape of Snoopy's doghouse, bars on the windows, the cracked asphalt parking lot a garden of spiked weeds, the sign above the entrance revealing the last remnant of some long gone business, *"bart"* in red script.

Inside was small and there were only a few shelves stocked with random single items—Ritz crackers, Saltines, a three-pack of sponges—while the refrigerated cases were fully stocked with soda, beer, malt liquor, wine coolers, and Gatorade. The counter was walled with thick glass and a bank drive-thru drawer.

Behind the glass was a large, bearded black man in a brown leisure shirt and fedora with feather, puffing a cigarillo, wearing sunglasses, standing in front of a stacked rack of Newports and Phillies Blunts.

"Clifford from Shopper's Village said I should see you," Griff said to the glass.

After three long days holed up in the executive conference room of Hammersmith Nuclear's headquarters negotiating with the French over the sale of twenty cooling systems for the country's network of nuclear power plants, followed by the uncorking of several vintage Bordeaux wines after the contracts were signed, Mike, with a headache from the wine and stinky French cigarette smoke, made the final turn down the cul-de-sac and pressed the button on the Radio Shack Realistic Remote Gate Opener.

Shirt undone, tie draped over shoulder, he ascended the marble platform steps up to the front door and went inside.

Joyce was on the living room couch smoking a cigarette and sipping burgundy. On the coffee table was a VHS cassette with the label peeled off.

"I bet you can't guess what's on the tape," she said, exhaling towards the ceiling.

"*Return of the Jedi*."

"Nope."

"*Raiders of the Lost Ark*."

"Nope."

"*E.T.*"

"No, I—"

"*Jaws*."

"Alright, stop—"

"*Annie Hall*."

"Mike, really—"

"The last episode of *M*A*S*H*."

"Stop!"

She took a deep breath, sipped the burgundy, stamped out the cigarette, then lit another.

"Let's just say I know how those girls at the airport recognized you—*Hammer*."

Mike smiled.

"Let me fix a drink, then I'll tell you everything."

He went to the minibar and poured himself a Johnnie Walker Red, neat, then took a seat next to Joyce and lit a cigarette.

"I always knew this might come up," he started, "and I apologize for keeping it a secret. I know that's like lying, but it's painful for me to think of that time in my life because it was so long ago, and I wrestled with whether I should just tell you, but I didn't want to scare you away. I was enjoying myself so much whenever I was with you, it just never seemed like the right moment. I was happier than I've ever been, and I still am. Originally, I thought this stuff would just go away over time, but the VCR brought it back to life. At pretty much any video store in the world, you can go behind the curtain in the back, and there's young me. Why do you think I grew the mustache? It actually works, because people know me from somewhere, and are usually satisfied to think they are confusing me with Burt Reynolds—except for hardcore fans like the ones at the airport, who've probably been watching porn since they were in diapers."

"Eww."

"Eww is right. But, back then, we were poor. My parents were immigrants from Sicily. They came here with nothing. They struggled when they got here, and my father refused the help being offered by some of the other Sicilians, and even some of our own family members, who had ties to *La Cosa Nostra*. And then I was born, and they struggled even more, but they believed in the dream of America, if not for them, then, at least for me. My father worked in a cannery in

Brooklyn and they paid him next to nothing, but we had food on the table every night in our little apartment, just the three of us. He was always adamant that I don't get mixed up with those *'hoodlums on the street corners'*. I knew some of those guys from school, but I didn't get mixed up in anything bad. I was a good student, on the Honor Roll, and I was accepted to every college I applied to. They gave me what little they had to send me to college, but it wasn't enough, not even close.

"Then, one night, I'm out with my buddies driving all over Brooklyn, we're bored and just looking for stuff to do, you know, stupid teenage stuff, and we stop at a diner just off the Belt Parkway. I go into the men's room to take a leak, and, while I'm peeing, some guy comes in and takes the urinal right next to me. I can tell the guy is looking at my thing, and, finally, I tell him to put his eyes back on the tiles or I'd pop him one. He does and he apologizes and says he's not a homo, but an adult film producer, and that he's always on the lookout for new talent. After we're done peeing, he hands me a business card and it's for something called L.I. 69 Studios somewhere out in Suffolk County. He says, 'You can make good money with that thing in your pants', and then he leaves. I don't know what to make of it and I'm still thinking the guy might be a perv, so I put the card in my pocket and forget about it.

"The days go by, I'm stocking shelves at the grocery store, and I know there's no way I'll ever be able to pay for college doing this, and I also want to help out my parents financially, but I'm not gonna get mixed up with the mob guys like some of my cousins already had. Then I find the card in my pocket. It takes a few days, but, finally, I work up the nerve to call the number and some woman answers and transfers me to the guy from the diner. His name is 'Val', and he turns out to be the head of the whole studio and invites me to come out there. I tell him I don't have a car and don't know where Centereach is, so he offers to send a car service and says he'll give me a hundred bucks just to come out and talk to him and see the studio. Again I'm thinking the guy's a perv, but a hundred bucks is a lot of money, and I figure I can just fight my way out if he tries anything.

"So, the next day, a black Cadillac picks me up in Sheepshead bay and the driver shows me the hundred bucks inside the envelope, but says he can't give it to me until we get out there. So I get in and the drive takes forever, and we're out in the middle of nowhere, nothing but farms and some new housing developments, until we pull up to this huge, unmarked warehouse building, and he drops me at the front door and hands me the envelope.

"He waits there when I go inside, and I'm really nervous, and the receptionist is beautiful, and she tells me to take a seat in the waiting area. I sit there for ten minutes trying not to look at her, but I can't help it, and I don't know what's happening, and I'm sweating, and I just want to tell them to forget about the hundred bucks and take me home. Then Val comes out, he's all smiles, and tells me to follow him. We go down a hall and wind up on one of the sets where they're shooting a movie, and there's a dozen gorgeous women standing around with incredible bodies, some of them nude, and a few naked men, and nobody cared, and he said they make several pictures a day, and that the actors get paid $500 for each one.

"So, how's a poor kid from Brooklyn supposed to say 'no' to this? A few cheesy lines, then make love to a beautiful woman? Ah, but there's where I learned the difference between having sex and making love. These women didn't care about me, and I didn't care about them. We all just wanted to get it done so we could get our money and go home. There was no passion in it. We had to act passionate, which is harder to do than it sounds, especially when you're surrounded by people and the director is telling you what to do—faster, slower, shoot the load already—and you're just thrown together with whoever's ready to go at the moment. There's nothing personal in it. I only had sex with those women. I make love to you."

She looked away.

"I still want to be mad," she said.

"But you're not."

"No. I understand now why you did it."

"But you're still upset."

"No."

"Then what is it?"

"I want you to shave your mustache and do to me what you did to that girl in the video."

Dusk at Birch Lane Elementary in Massapequa, the last of the teachers and principal gone for the day, the parking lot empty.

On the cafeteria side of the building's exterior was a six-foot high brick wall, behind which were stored several stacks of empty plastic milk crates, brown ones, from Liberty Farms.

Griff had already bungee-corded a crate to his handlebars, a blue one from Honeywell Farms, that Bart had given him and told him to say, if anyone asked, was for his paper route. The stripped-down Huffy had no kickstand, so he leaned it against the wall and took two of the Liberty Farms crates, placing one sideways inside the Honeywell crate, then covering it with the other Liberty Farms facing bottom up. He took three more Liberty Farms and configured them the same way atop the other three, then secured them into a tight bundle with bungee cords from the dozen in his backpack.

Riding with the tower of plastic in front of his face, he was able to see well enough through the spaces in the crates to navigate, though steering with the extra weight took some getting used to. Heading east on the backroads south of Merrick Road, he stayed off the main thoroughfare except when a canal or some other extension of the Great South Bay required it, through Nassau Shores, past the Nautilus Diner and Berner High School, into Far East Massapequa, and over the border, before turning north.

At *Executives Gentleman's Lounge* on Route 110 in Melville —

Larry Teat, CEO of Hammersmith Nuclear, looked at the Finnish officials with whom they'd just inked the biggest contract in the history of the company, much thanks to the efforts of his Executive VP of Sales, Mike Ramone, to whom he turned and asked over the loud music, "Do you think they're having a good time?"

Mike looked at the Finns staring into their vodka-blueberry juices, surrounded by five of *Executives'* top-rated topless dancers trying to get their attention.

"If you look closely, they're nodding a little. See? Look at Mustanen over there."

"I gotta hand it to you, Mike, it was looking iffy for a while until you pulled it together. At best it was looking like another two or three days with these guys."

"That's what lit the fire under my ass this afternoon."

"Gonna be a hell of a bonus this year."

Behind the Bart Mart—

"These are sweet," Bart said, inspecting the five Liberty Farms milk crates Griff had just brought him. "I'll give you two-fifty apiece and throw in a 40 of ice cold Colt 45 and a pack of Newports."

Griff, hands on knees, out of breath, shook his head.

"Two-fifty apiece, two Miller High Life, and a pack of Blunts."

"Damn, G! Clifford said you a hustler. Alright, alright. Just keep bringing me these motherfuckers, and if you see any olive green Queensboros with the yellow lettering, I'll give you four apiece for those. If you see any orange ones, they super rare, I'll give you ten apiece for those. Dellwoods, Honeywells, gray Queensboros, three apiece. Liberty, Dairylea, two-fifty."

"How much for Sunnydales?"

"Those beige ones they have a million of behind FoodTown?"

"Yeah."

"Dollar-fifty. And three-fifty for Dairy Barns. Those are hard to get because those places never close, but I already got a guy over here who gets those. You gotta get to know the guy who works the night shift to score those motherfuckers."

On the patio, blue sky, hot coffee, burning cigarette, Joyce watched the sailboat glide across the glistening Great South Bay and something began to stir. Minutes later, she was in the garage digging through U-Haul boxes marked "Joyce Painting Stuff".

She set up on the patio, the gentle breeze from the water now blowing harder, the breakers down on the beach louder and more frequent, a carpet of gray clouds consuming the sky. By the time brush finally stroked canvas, the sailboat was gone.

Landscapes were never her thing, nor were sailboats. A large raindrop hit the canvas. She needed another cigarette, and maybe a glass of wine, but it wasn't even noon. A gust of wind knocked the canvas off the easel. A streak of lightning split the horizon. The darker landscape inspired her anew, but it began to pour. By the time she got everything back into the house, she and her supplies and cigarettes were soaked, and the paint was mixing with the rainwater and dripping everywhere.

It was quarter past noon when she'd finally finished cleaning the mess. Not bothering with lunch, she uncorked a bottle of burgundy and spent the afternoon in front of the bay window with the wine and a fresh pack of cigarettes, storm raging across the backyard sea, no sailboats, and no rainbows when it was over, just a brightening of the gray sky and a calming of the water.

Griff turned the Huffy onto the cul-de-sac and saw "Uncle Jimmy" waiting in front of the driveway gate.

"Hey, kid."

"Hey, Uncle Jimmy. What are you doing out here?"

"I need to talk to you about that thing."

"What thing?"

"That crate thing."

"Uh-oh."

"That's right, *uh-oh*. You know whose turf you've been stealing those on, don't you?"

"How do you even know about this?"

"I know about everything that goes down around here."

"Are you like Don Corleone?"

"More like Tessio."

"Shit."

"Yeah, that's right, *shit*. But it's okay, kid, as long as you do the right thing."

"Okay, Uncle Jimmy. I'll stop stealing crates."

"No, kid, you misunderstand me. You can steal all the crates you want. In fact, I implore you to steal more. You just have to give me my piece. *Capisci?*"

"*Capisci*," Griff said, reaching into his pocket.

"And next time, bring it in an envelope. It doesn't have to be anything fancy, just a regular white envelope. Maybe gently wrinkled so it's a little soft."

"Okay, Uncle Jimmy."

At the Flynt mansion, two days after the New York Mets' Game 7 victory over the Boston Red Sox, the World Series trophy on the kitchen counter, Mike working the keg of Bud filling the players' mugs—

"Hey, Mikey," one of them said, "care to join us downstairs in the rec room for a little—"

The player pointed at his nose.

Mike looked out the window at Joyce alone on the deck sipping a margarita across the empty pool from Bobby Darin and his band.

"Sure," he said.

In a distant guest room—

"Your mouth tastes like tobacco juice," Dolly said, between kisses.

"Is it bothering you?" the player asked.

"No, I like it."

"Good," he said, looking sweetly into her eyes, his face smeared with makeup, " 'cause that's what I'm gonna make your pussy taste like."

Kitchen vacated, Fred looked out the window, then went out to the deck, glancing at Joyce while approaching Bobby Rydell on the other side of the pool—

"Hey, Bobby," he said, pulling a wad of cash from his

pocket, "why don't you and the boys call it a night."

"Thanks, Fred," Bobby said, then turned to the band and said, "Come on, guys, let's scram."

Fred turned when he heard the sliding door open and watched Joyce, now inside, slide it closed and lock it.

Down in Fred's rec room —

"Mike?" a woman's voice called from the top of the stairs. "Mike, are you down there?"

"Mike, are you down there?" one of the players mocked, prompting a round of laughter.

"I'll be up in a minute," Mike called back.

"Alright, but hurry up. I'll be out in the car."

The door at the top of the stairs closed.

"Hurry up, I'll be out in the car," another player mocked, and everyone laughed.

"You guys mind if I get one more for the road?" Mike asked, laughing with the others.

Griff, pedaling east on the shoulder of Sunrise Highway with five orange Gowanus Farms crates on the handlebars, just short of the border, heard the siren behind him and slowed to a stop.

Straddling the frame, he waited as the Nassau County Police Officer stepped out of the cruiser and, hand on piece, cautiously approached.

"Step off the bike," he ordered.

"It doesn't have a kickstand," Griff said. "It's gonna fall if I get off."

"What happened to the kickstand?"

"I took it off."

"Why would you do something stupid like that?"

"Because I wanted too."

"Alright, then, Joe Cool. Let it fall and put your hands behind your head and spread your legs apart."

Griff lifted his leg over the frame, then let go of the hand grip. Before bike and crates hit the asphalt, he was sprinting towards County Line Road, darting through honking traffic, to the southeast corner, where he watched the winded officer pull to a stop across the street.

Before continuing to Route 110, Griff, both middle fingers extended, shouted over the passing traffic, "Fuck you, pig!"

His name was Eli Jones and the cover of The Smith's *Meat Is Murder* was patched to the back of his leather jacket, his hair dyed black, Doc Marten boots, black jeans, silver earrings in both ears.

Stacy, on her way to the bus after last period, passed his locker every day, but never once did he look.

Sometimes he was alone, and sometimes he was talking to his friend, Damian, who, today, was there asking if he wanted to hang out after school.

"I can't," Eli said, "I have confirmation class."

"Confirmation? I've never seen you at confirmation."

"I go to Our Savior's Grace."

"Our Savior's Grace? What the hell is that?"

"A Lutheran Church."

At the Bart Mart—

"I can't do this anymore," Griff said to Bart, on the other side of the glass puffing a Phillie.

"You sure you don't feel that way after just missing your golden score and losing your ride?"

"Nah. I'm too big for the Huffy, and, at this point, I could just get a job at FoodTown and make more money a few hours a night without all the stress and riding."

"Alright, I hear ya, G, but this a sad day for me 'cause you the best crate hustler I ever seen, even better than my Dairy Barn guy. You right, though, milk crates a minor league business, and you ready for the big leagues. And you just give me an idea, something perfect for you."

"As long as bicycles aren't involved."

"No bikes, G. All you gotta do is sit there."

"You want to go to confirmation class?" her mother asked, eyebrows raised, lighting a cigarette.

Stacy nodded.

"Well, this is a pleasant surprise, especially after you and your brother were expelled from Sunday School back in West Hempstead."

Stacy shrugged.

"Well, alright then. I'll call Pastor Michael."

In the Executive Washroom at Hammersmith Nuclear global headquarters—

Mike, in a stall, having just snorted a line of cocaine from the back of his hand through a twenty dollar bill, a bigger line than his nostril could handle, the excess falling into his mustache and the toilet, wiped his nose with the back of his hand, unaware of the powder in his stache and that his nose was bleeding, and that he'd just smeared both all over his left cheek.

He was also unaware that, during his snort, Mr. Hayashi, from 日本原子力研究所, the Japan Atomic Energy Research Institute, one of a dozen officials from Tokyo they'd been negotiating with for the past 36 hours over parts for Japan's aging power plants—very expensive parts, reactor vessels, control rods, vapor generators, turbines, alternators, reactor vessels, pumps, condensers, the whole schmear—had entered the washroom, and was now at one of the sinks staring at him in the mirror.

"Howdy, Mr. Hayashi," Mike said, smiling.

Mr. Hayashi did not return the pleasantry and swiftly exited the washroom.

Mike looked at himself in the mirror.

"Shit!" he exclaimed, turning on the water and rinsing the mess off his face as his left nostril continued to bleed. He went back to the stall and pulled some toilet paper that he twisted and stuffed into the bleeding nostril, then rinsed his face again and washed his hands before hurrying back to the Executive Conference room, where alone sat CEO Larry Teat smoking a Marlboro Light.

"Where'd they go?" Mike asked.

"Well, Mr. Hayashi came back from the washroom claiming to have witnessed you snorting cocaine in the toilet stall, and that you had blood and powder all over your face. Then he said, 'We refuse to do business with your John Belushi,' and then they all filed out and climbed into those Continentals waiting out front and pulled away."

"Jesus Christ."

"Is it true, Mike?"

He looked down at the table. "Yeah. It's true."

"Are you a drug addict, Mike?"

"No, Larry, of course not."

"No?"

"No. I'll stop, though. It won't happen again. I just needed it for the Japanese, 36 hours, I was tired—"

"You're lying, Mike."

"No, Lar—"

"You need help."

"Larry, please, let me explain—"

"You're fired, Mike. Go clean out your office, then go get yourself cleaned up."

At Eli Jones' locker—

"Dude, that weirdo freak girl showed up at my confirmation class yesterday," said Eli to Damian.

"You mean the one who just walked by?"

Both boys looked at her, she turning away.

"That's the one," Eli said.

Inside the FoodTown frozen foods locker, at the moment smelling as if inhabited by a family of Arctic skunks—

Griff, bundled in puffy winter coat and knitted Dallas Cowboys cap with pom-pom on top, seated on a stack of tan Sunnydale crates, looked up when the vaultlike door opened behind the heavy rubber flaps.

"You got a customer," said Lou, the frozen foods night guy, who then began pulling out a cart loaded with Gorton's Fish Sticks, Gabila's Coney Island Potato Knishes, Eggo Waffles, and Breyer's Ice Cream.

Griff nodded, and in stepped a guy he knew from school.

"I just need a dime," the guy said.

From his coat pocket Griff produced a dime bag so fat with L.A. EndoChronic it wouldn't close.

The guy handed him two wrinkled five dollar bills and said, "Thanks, G."

"Tell your homies, J."

In the drawing his back was turned, his smirking face looking over his shoulder, *Meat Is Murder* patch on leather jacket, black jeans, Doc Marten boots, silver earrings—

She flipped the lid on the Crayola 64 box and pulled a virgin from the dedicated Brick Red section, then double-X'd him out.

Pastor Michael, in his office at Our Savior's Grace, hearing the scream, sprung from his Corinthian leather executive chair and hurried to the Youth Wing—

"Susan, what is it?" he asked, finding the trembling youth in the Copy/Office Supply/Bible Packet Room, in front of "The Great Wall" of custom-built cubbies housing the Bible packet worksheets for the confirmation students, each packet around 6-10 double-sided pages containing reading passages and review questions, some also containing special group projects, roadblocks, and detours to be completed before confirmand can proceed to the "Pit Stop" on the last page, a different packet for each Bible book, Old and New Testaments, each a unique color, the pastor having splurged on the fluorescent and special order colors at Staples to make this possible.

In her hand was the plain white *Genesis* packet with Brick Red "X" drawn across the cover sheet, and every page that followed, front and back. The other *Genesis* copies in the cubby were also X'd out—goldenrod *Exodus*, azure *Leviticus*, Kodiak grey *Numbers*, salmon pink *Ruth*, tangerine dream *Habakkuk*, and the New Testament packets, canary yellow *Corinthians 1 & 2*, fig leaf green *Jude*, crimson *Revelation*—

"Who could have done this without anyone noticing?" asked Pastor Michael, randomly pulling packets from The Great Wall, all X'd out. "This would have taken... I don't know, days? And how many Brick Red crayons? Is it a sign, Susan? Have we been paid a visit by The Evil One?"

At the home of Tony and Marie Scarpellini in Oceanside, NY—

"Amen," said Tony Sr., retired FDNY Captain, after Marie finished saying grace, the Thanksgiving feast spread before him and the fifteen adult family members seated around the quadruple-leafed table, the men FDNY firefighters, the women homemakers. At the kiddie folding tables, the boys resumed their lively conversation about dinosaurs, and the girls bragged about the weddings they would someday have and what their firefighter husbands would look like.

Marie looked at her daughter, Theresa, and smiled. Theresa smiled back, then looked at her husband, Oscar, and smiled. Oscar smiled back, then looked at his mother in-law and smiled. She smiled back, then looked at her daughter and smiled.

The men had radios strapped to their belts, all of them volunteer firefighters in Oceanside, and all of them owning houses on this same block. Tony Sr. had a radio unit on top of the China cabinet, which, along with everyone's radios, began to beep, then a staticky voice came through all the speakers, *"Two alarm in Rockville Centre, may need backup."*

The boys continued to eat. Tony Jr., having just finished one of the drumsticks from the 30 pound turkey, reached for the lasagna.

"This is Baldwin, we got two guys comin'," said someone on the radio.

"You gonna get that call?" Tony Sr. asked, looking from son to son.

"Nah, they got it, Pop," Frankie finally said, chewing.

"It's Thanksgiving, they might be a little light."

"Give it a minute and see if they need anyone," said Tony Jr.

"I'll go," Oscar said, wiping gravy from his chin with a cloth napkin.

"Take a seat, showoff," Jimmy said.

"Yous oughta take a lesson," said Tony Sr., pointing his butter knife at each of his sons.

"Actually," Oscar said, "it wouldn't be a bad idea for me to step away from all this delicious food before I get fat again."

"You're too thin," said his mother in-law.

"Why don't yous all go," said Tony Sr., "then, when yous get back, we'll have coffee and cake."

"Okay, Pop," Tony Jr. said, then to the others, "Come on, we'll take my van."

The VHS tape had been wrapped in brown grocery bag paper and addressed to her in black block lettering.

The label was peeled off and the tape was not rewound.

She brought it to the bedroom, closed the door, and put it in the VCR. The footage was new and high quality, like soap operas. There was a woman on a couch in a living room, a blonde around her own age. The doorbell rang. She answered it.

"Howdy, babe."

"Sonny—"

It was Mike, not looking a day younger than when he'd left the house that morning, wearing a white linen suit, teal t-shirt, white deck shoes without socks, Ray-Bans—

"Oh, God—"

The woman invited him in. They got undressed and

started having sex. Then the front door flew open and in burst a fat, mustached man in a red Hawaiian shirt and baseball cap, who pointed his gun at them and yelled, *"Freeze!"*

"Oh, God—"

"Howdy, Mugnam!" Sonny exclaimed, still fucking the woman. *"Care to join in?"*

"Come join us, Terry," said the woman, between moans.

Phil Collins-like music started to play. Mugnam lowered his gun and got undressed. He had a big one too. He went over and the woman started using her mouth on him, at which point Joyce forwarded to the credits.

Hammer Vice, starring The Hammer as Sonny Hammer. Written and Directed by The Hammer. None of the other names were recognizable. © Copyright 1989, LI 69 Studios. FBI anti-piracy warning.

Inside the FoodTown frozen foods locker—

"There's a really scary old dude out there," Lou said to Griff.

"Is it a cop?"

"More like Mafia."

"Shit," Griff said. "Is his name Jimmy and does he have a mustache?"

"I didn't get his name, but he does have a mustache."

"Alright, send him in."

Lou opened the door and Uncle Jimmy stepped through the heavy rubber flaps.

"Griff, what the fuck?"

"I was gonna tell you, Uncle Jimmy, but I haven't seen you—"

"I oughta lock you in here and let you freeze with the TV dinners!"

"Here, look, I've been setting aside your piece, this is all of it."

Griff produced a gently wrinkled envelope from inside his puffy coat and handed it to him.

"This is nice," Uncle Jimmy said, looking in the envelope. "Alright, you done good, kid. Keep it up."

"Thanks, Uncle Jimmy."

On the kitchen counter was a VHS tape with the label stripped off, but he walked right by it on his way to the liquor cabinet—

"Mike!"

"Not now, hon. I'm really tired."

"I know you know what's on that tape."

"Please, not now."

"Yes, now. Start explaining."

He sipped his Johnnie Walker, then looked at the floor tiles.

"What's the matter? Need some extra time coming up with one of your smooth explanations, Mr. Smooth?"

Finally he looked at her.

"I need help," he said.

Behind the wheel of his brick red '78 Volkswagen Rabbit, the new Public Enemy *Fear of a Black Planet* in the tape deck, subwoofers pumping bass that could be heard on the other side of the Southern State Parkway, Griff rolled into his spot behind the Bart Mart.

The back screen door of the bodega flew open and hit the cinder block wall.

"Yo, motherfucker!" Bart shouted, Phillie in hand. "Knock that shit off!"

"You don't like P.E.?" Griff asked, getting out of the car.

"Chuck D is bad for business. Motherfucker says the shit I sell in my store is exploiting black people, which I take exception to. I'm just a brother makin' a livin' in the white man's country, and I'm simply providing what some of the black people want. If you don't want that shit in yo house, than mind yo own business, motherfucker. Some people want it, and it better to just let them have it, and let another brother make a living. And you watch out, he gonna put some bad ideas in yo head with that Farrakhan shit."

"Don't worry, I'm not the religious type. But I don't want to sell weed anymore."

"Is sittin' in that freezer chillin' yo brain?"

"No. I don't mind smoking tea, but I don't like selling it."

"*Tea*? What the fuck is that shit, 'tea'?"

"That's what Kerouac calls it."

"Who the fuck Kerr-ack?"

"Jack Kerouac, he's a writer. He wrote *On the Road*. He's dead now."

"How you gonna earn if you ain't sellin' no tea?"

"I wanna learn how to play guitar and write songs."

"What? For real? You have been in that motherfucker freezer too long, G. You ain't gonna make no money that way."

"That's okay. I just wanna learn. And I don't want to get

busted. I want to go to college."

"College? What the fuck you gonna do there?"

"I don't know. Join a frat. Drink beer. Meet girls."

"Shit, you turnin' pale on me, motherfucker."

"I didn't say I was leaving the game. I just don't wanna sell weed anymore."

"Alright, I get it. I'll get someone else to take over yo FoodTown shit. I got something else for you anyway that even Chuck D wouldn't object to."

Behind the wheel of her white E-Class, heading east on the L.I.E. towards the Rocky Point Rehabilitation Center, LITE-FM on the stereo, "Sailing" by Christopher Cross, Joyce said to Mike, next to her in the passenger seat staring out the window, "This is a good thing. You're doing the right thing. You can stay however long you need, relax, get clean, and, when you get out, you can talk to Larry about getting your job back."

Mike didn't respond.

"I know this is hard," she said. "It's hard for me too."

"I'm sorry for putting you through this," he finally said.

"That's okay. You're sick, and now they're going to make you well."

She looked at him, waiting for a response.

"Yeah," he eventually mumbled.

Just outside the frozen foods locker at Waldbaum's—

"Twenty," Griff said to a guy he knew from school.

The guy produced a combination of currency that included a pair of crisp, gift-card ready two-dollar bills.

"Alright, listen up, B, 'cause you gotta follow the rules," said Griff, pocketing the cash, sporting a pair of new Adidas Superstars with silver stripes and a 1977 Seattle Mariners trident cap. "As soon as you go in, you're on the clock. Her name is Thelma, and be respectful and polite. Just tell her whether you want a hand or a blow, those are the only things on the menu. As soon as the clock starts, you have five minutes, whether you finish or not. And don't try anything funny or be disrespectful. She has a panic button that will page the beeper belonging to that big security guard you passed on the way in. If she presses it, Tiny's gonna come back here and you're gonna have to deal with him, so don't try anything. Got it?"

"Got it, G."

"Alright, B, go in, and, as soon as this door closes, you're on the clock. Thanks for your business and tell your homies. Peace in the Middle East."

At the Sunrise Mall Military Career Center, the ringing phone was answered by—

"Lieutenant Dwight Hampton, Unites States Navy. How may I assist you?"

"Hey, Dwight, it's Bill Zimbardo over at the high school."

"Hey, Bill. How's my favorite guidance counselor?"

"I'm doin' alright."

"Got any good ones for me?"

"Sure, this is a good one. Name is Griffin Ramsey. C

student. Long hair. Listens to rap music, if you would even call that 'music'. Going nowhere. Didn't take the practice SATs, so I'm assuming he's not even thinking about college. If you want to swing by, I'll show you his file and yearbook photo, and I've got a few other good prospects."

"Sounds good, Bill, I'll stop by tomorrow around noon. Go Navy!"

"Go Navy," Bill said, then hung up.

In front of the main entrance of the Rocky Point Rehabilitation Center—

Joyce, behind the wheel of the parked E-Class, lit another cigarette, then resumed watching people passing through the building's automatic sliding doors, some in wheelchairs, LITE-FM on the stereo, Dan Fogelberg's "Same Old Lang Syne", until Mike emerged from the din wearing the same clothes now rumpled and a pair of glasses she'd never seen, appearing heavier and healthier.

He opened the passenger door and got in.

"Are you clean?" she asked.

"Yeah, I'm clean. They made it clear I would have been dead within a year if I'd kept doing that stuff, so, yes, I'm done with it for good. Now let's get the hell out of here so I can have a drink."

At the Sunrise Mall Military Career Center—

From his desk, Lt. Dwight Hampton spotted the mark

walking by out on the concourse, but waited a moment before getting up and following. He passed JCPenney, Spencer Gifts, Herman's Sporting Goods, and Friendly's, before suddenly turning around.

Lt. Hampton stepped in front of him.

"Excuse me, son," he said. "Are you hungry? Do you need something to eat?"

"Get the fuck away from me, asshole," the mark said.

"No need for hostility, son. I just noticed you walking back and forth in front of Friendly's and thought you'd enjoy a nice hot meal and some ice cream for dessert. They make a mean cod melt here, and, for dessert, I recommend either the Reese's Pieces Sundae with Butter Crunch ice cream or the Watermelon Roll. How does that sound, son?"

"By nature I'm a Dharma pacifist, but, if you call me 'son' again, I'm gonna knock your teeth clear to JCPenney."

At the hostess lectern inside Friendly's—

"Dwight is such a tool," said Janine, the hostess, to D'arcy, the waitress, after witnessing the encounter out on the concourse.

"The longhaired guy's been here a few times. He always orders the cheeseburger deluxe and doesn't like coleslaw, so he gets double fries and gets like five or six Coke refills."

"He looks like a strawberry Fribble kind of guy."

"No. Banana split with pistachio ice cream."

"That sounds like something a ninety year-old would order."

"Send him to my section if he comes in," D'arcy said, then went into the kitchen.

At Hammersmith Nuclear global headquarters—

Larry Teat heard the engine roar and looked out his corner office window at the rusted Trans Am pulling into one of the visitor parking spots.

Mike got out and waved. Larry waved back. Moments later, the former Executive VP of Sales was in the office.

"Good to see you, Mike," Larry said, extending his hand. "You look well. Healthy."

"Thanks, you too. How are things with you?"

"Can't complain. Well, I can, but who'd listen."

"Yeah."

"So, they got you clean out there in Rocky Point?"

"Yeah. They did a good job. I couldn't have done it alone."

"That's good, Mike, glad to hear it. That's the most important thing, your health."

"Yes, it is. And my health has improved greatly, and now I just need to get back to work and keep myself busy."

"So, what are you thinking about doing next?"

"Well, Larry, I was hoping to come back here."

"I was afraid you'd say that."

"Larry, I know I messed up, and for that I am deeply sorry, but I'm clean now, and I'm more focused than I've been in a long time, and I'd start at a lower level—"

"I believe you, Mike, and I wish I could help. But the board has made it clear they want nothing to do with you, and, in fact, they probably wouldn't even appreciate me sitting here talking to you. I'm sorry, Mike, but your reputation is in the toilet right now. I had lunch with some guys from Grumman last week and they heard rumors that you were holed up in a Hollywood bungalow shooting speedballs."

"Come on, Larry, you know me—"

"Sorry, Mike, there's nothing I can do. My hands are tied."

At Friendly's—

D'arcy approached the table and said, "Cheeseburger deluxe, no coleslaw, double fries, Coke, banana split with pistachio ice cream."

The longhaired guy looked up from his menu.

"Whoa," he said.

"Why do you even bother looking at the menu?"

"Because they keep giving me one."

"I saw what happened out there with Dwight."

"Who?"

"Lieutenant Hampton? The Navy recruiter who was harassing you?"

"Is that an apostrophe or a scratch on your nametag?"

"It's an apostrophe. Don't ask."

"I like apostrophes."

"You do?"

"They're underrated. And so are Oxford commas. So, is it pronounced *'Dah-arcy'*, or is it just *'Darcy'*?"

"Silent apostrophe."

"Far out. Maybe I should put an apostrophe in my name. But it wouldn't be silent."

"What's your name?"

"Griffin, but nobody calls me that. Everyone calls me 'Griff' or 'G'."

"Can I call you 'Griffin'?"

The doorbell rang during *The People's Court*.

Joyce put down her burgundy and wandered towards the door, trying to hear Judge Wapner's decision, until the doorbell rang again.

"Alright, I'm coming."

She pulled open the door.

"Oh, hi, sailor," she said to the tall young man in the Navy uniform. "Can I help you?"

"Are you the mother of Griffin Ramsey, ma'am?"

"Uh, yes. Is he in trouble?"

"He will be if he continues down the road he's on, but I would be happy to discuss with you some possible career paths for your son in the United States Navy. He might think it's not cool, but this isn't your daddy's Navy. We're cool now."

"Oh," she said, looking at the glossy brochures and pamphlets he was holding of fighter jets, aircraft carriers, and the Dallas Cowboys Cheerleaders at a USO Tour stop, along with several *GO NAVY* bumper stickers.

"I'm Lieutenant Dwight, Hampton, ma'am, and if I could have just five minutes of your time, I can discuss with you what it would mean for Griffin to choose a career path in the United States Navy, and I can leave these materials with you to go over with him. It may save his life, ma'am."

"Oh, uh, well, sure, okay, come on in."

Inside the frozen foods locker at Waldbaum's—

On a bed made of bags of Birds Eye frozen peas stacked on a pallet in the corner, nude inside the sleeping bag earlier purchased at Herman's Sporting Goods, Griff kissed D'Arcy—

"I love you," he said.

"What? Oh, Griffin, no—"

"I've never met a woman like you."

"I have a kid."

"A what?"

"A kid. A son. Brandon. He's two."

"Whoa."

"Yeah, *whoa*. Don't get me wrong, Griffin, I like you, you're a nice kid, but you're still in high school, and we just met. I'm already a divorced mother."

"I don't have anything against divorced mothers."

"But you're too young to fall in love with one, and, if I'm going to fall in love with someone, he needs to be steady. He doesn't have to be rich, or even the most handsome guy, but I need—Brandon and I need someone steady. A nine-to-five kind of guy. Has a job in an office park. Barbecues with family and neighbors on the weekend."

"That's really what you want?"

"It is now. Not long ago I was planning on going to college, then traveling the world, Europe, Australia, Asia, then living in Manhattan for a while, in the Village, then eventually getting married someday, like, in my thirties. Then Brandon came along. I didn't even get to go to college."

"You're bummin' me out, D-pos."

"That's because you still want to do things like that. Of course, I was bummed out at first, and had a few bouts of depression, but I don't care about that stuff anymore. Brandon is my life now."

"You're like Mary in 'The River'."

"Who?"

"The Springsteen song. She was just living her life, hanging out down at the river with her boyfriend, and then he got her pregnant, and then everything that mattered suddenly didn't matter anymore, and then it was just marriage and jobs and the economy and then, I don't know—"

"Life?"

"Yeah. Just some boring old life. That's all she wrote."

"I'm okay with being Mary. But you wouldn't be okay being Mary's husband, and you wouldn't be okay living some boring old life on Long Island. You don't belong here, Griffin. You have to go find the place where *you* belong."

"This is an impressive résumé, Mike," said Charlie McAdoo, Human Resources Director at LILCO, the Long Island Lighting Company, "but this isn't anything like the jet set world of international nukes. We just need a parts buyer for our facilities. It's a hectic, thankless job that's never done, because someone always needs something."

"I was burnt out from that life anyway," Mike said. "I need a change. Something a little quieter."

Charlie looked at the résumé again.

"Alright, Mike. We've got a few more candidates coming in, but we'll keep you in mind and give you a call if we want you back for a second interview."

Just arrived home, Griff went into the kitchen where, on the counter, lay an organized display of glossy brochures, pamphlets, and *GO NAVY* bumper stickers—

"What the fuck is this shit?" he asked just as his mother appeared, in her robe, holding a glass of wine.

"How was work?" she asked.

"Where the fuck did this shit come from?"

"It's not shit, Griff. Just look at it. The Navy is cool now."

"Where'd you get it?"

"Well, a nice man from the recruiting office stopped by, Lieutenant Hampton—"

"Motherfucker," he said, then went up to his room.

At LaSalle Park in Buffalo, New York—

"So, I'm going to stand right here," said the host of *The Reverend Virgil Marvin Show*, scheduled to premiere Friday night at 10:00 on Community Access Channel 79, "and my four Torchbearers will stand behind me, two on either side."

The reverend, age 45, lanky, pale skin, dyed black hair slicked back, curly mustache and waxed goatee, black satin shirt and pants, black satin cape with red interior, ordained by the Church of Satan, the official one, waited for a response from the cameraman, Frank, an overweight community college student wearing a black satin Community Access Channel 79 jacket over a blue #12 Jim Kelly jersey.

"Wait," Frank finally said. "What about lighting? There aren't any lights in this part of the park, and it's gonna be dark as hell at 10:00, and the only light is gonna be from those little Home Depot torches?"

"There will be a spotlight on me, but each of the four Torchbearers will be holding a torch before them so their faces will be lit by the flame, and they will be wearing black, so only their faces will be seen. The rest of it is supposed to look 'dark as hell'."

"Yeah. Yeah, that'll work. It'll look pretty cool on TV."

"Cool?"

"Sure. And you're just gonna be reading stuff out of that little book?"

"This 'little book'," said the reverend, holding up a pocket-sized journal with textured crimson cover, "contains passages drawn from the knowledge of a thousand lifetimes, knowledge I will use to awaken the minds and souls of those being forced against their will to live in this God-infected place."

"Buffalo?"

"The world in general."

"Planet Earth?"

"Yes."

"Are they, like, sleeping now?"

"Conscious suburban hibernation. CSH, for short."

"I never heard of that."

"Yes, well, not everyone will understand my wisdom, and you are probably one of those people."

"That's okay. I'm Jewish."

"Family religious background has nothing to do with it. My words connect only with people on a certain wavelength, and those people come from every creed you can imagine. We are not exclusionary."

"That's very progressive."

"At the end of the program, the Torchbearers will cast a vote to sacrifice one of their own."

"Sacrifice? Like human sacrifice?"

"No. They will vote one of themselves off and not come back on the program next week."

"Oh. Will there be a new Torchbearer?"

"Yes."

"And then one of those four will be voted off?"

"Yes. And we will also have a segment where we take live telephone calls, displaying a graphic with the caller's name and location, like on *Larry King Live*. We have a van full of video production equipment and a telephone switchboard."

"Cool. So, the show starts at ten on Friday night, maybe I'll get here around nine?"

"Yes. Be here at nine. At precisely ten pm, the enlightening will begin."

Behind the wheel of his taupe Ford Taurus, Lt. Dwight Hampton turned onto his block in Seaford but stopped short when he saw a black Oldsmobile 98 parked in his bungalow driveway.

"What the heck?" he wondered aloud.

Suddenly he was blinded by lights in the rearview mirror and the roar of four more black Olds 98s blocking him in.

The doors opened and out stepped a unit of AK-bearing African American men in black paramilitary uniforms. From the 98 in the driveway, out stepped a man in a red beret, while the man in the Pittsburgh Pirates cap behind the wheel and the man wearing the kitchen clock around his neck riding shotgun remained in the vehicle.

The man in the red beret approached the Taurus.

Lt. Hampton lowered the window.

"Evening," he said. "Care for a fry? I just stopped at All American Burger."

"You leave my boy Griff alone."

"Griff?"

"Don't act like you don't know who I'm talkin' about. Griff don't want no part of yo shit."

He raised a finger and the uniformed men clicked their weapons.

"Sir, you do realize I'm an officer in the United States Navy?"

"We know who you are, motherfucker. Just leave Griff alone, and we'll leave you alone."

Harry "Hangman" Hillman, in his driveway washing the white '86 DeVille he'd purchased after the record sales year at the business he and his late brother Hal started in 1961, Hillman Bros. Hanger Mfg., Co., Inc., halted the power nozzle when he saw his neighbor, Mike, in new suit and looking much better than the last time he'd seen him, albeit older and grayer, heading across the cul-de-sac towards him.

"What does this playboy want?" he muttered, then looked back at his wife, Phyllis, peeking through the living room curtains.

"Howdy, Harry," Mike said, smiling. "How's the hanger trade?"

"Can't complain. How are things in the nukes game?"

"Not so great, actually. The industry's been struggling since Chernobyl, and it's only gotten worse since *The Simpsons*.

Hammersmith laid a lot of us off a while back, including me."

"Sorry to hear it."

"Yeah, well, it's been rough. Nobody in nuclear is hiring, so I'm pretty much open to anything at this point. Maybe something with a little less travel. Local. A local business would be nice."

"Local? Really?"

"Sure. Something close to home."

"Say, Mike, I just had a crazy thought."

"What's that, Har?"

"Why don't you come work for me? I know the hanger business is probably below your speed, but I'm always looking for skilled salesmen, and I haven't been able to fill the northeast Nassau quadrant since ol' Biff retired. And, hell, maybe the rest of the team can pick up some pointers from a hotshot like you. Interested?"

"Sounds terrific, Har."

The illegal cable box her brother had sold her for ten bucks was open, Stacy meticulously turning the small metal channel rings on the motherboard that, when touching the exact spots, would get free HBO, Cinemax, Showtime, The Playboy Channel, SportsChannel, and several hundred community access stations and closed circuit horse track feeds across the United States—

"Good evening, Buffalo, or, as I call it, 'The coldest part of hell', ah-ah-ah."

She stopped turning and looked up at the man on the TV with the pointy goatee and curly mustache, red beads in black pupils, pale skin aglow, black satin garments with cape, and, behind him, four orange faces floating in front of torches—

"*I am the Reverend Virgil Marvin, and you, my disaffected viewer, are the lonely, the scared, the bored, the disgusted. I am here to inform those of you who may not know, and remind those of you who do, that your parents, and the inhabitants of Earth, have been brainwashing you since birth.*"

He put on a pair of reading glasses and held up a textured crimson pocket journal from which he began flipping through the pages.

"*Let us begin with a passage from* The Book of Belial, *and, afterwards, we'll take some phone calls before the sacrifice,*" he said, then began to read.

In a cold, damp Seattle rehearsal space, standing around a boom box listening to a demo tape—

"This guy's rockin'," one of the guys said.

"This is the surfer dude?"

"Yeah."

"What's he saying?"

"Something about still being alive."

"I got that part."

"He's a good singer. He's even better than the Long Island dude."

"I liked 'The Milk Crate Song', though."

"Well, let's get the surfer dude up here, and, if he doesn't work out, we'll try the Long Island dude."

At the Sunrise Mall Military Career Center—

"Excuse me," Joyce said to a woman in green camouflage, the only person on duty, "will Lieutenant Hampton be in today?"

"Lieutenant Hampton has transferred to a different station, ma'am."

"What? Where?"

"He's now stationed at the Fifth Avenue Mall Military Career Center in Anchorage, Alaska, ma'am."

"Alaska?"

"That's correct, ma'am. Anchorage, Alaska, ma'am."

"I have to admit," said Harry Hillman to Phyllis, his wife of thirty years, "I was more than a little nervous about hiring him, but he's already bringing in more new business than all the other salesmen combined. Granted, the Ramones are a little flaky—I guess you have to be to live in a house like that, especially with all that happened there—"

"He's related to them somehow," Phyllis said. "And I heard that he used to be on soap operas. And she's just a whore."

"Phyllis!"

"I'm sorry, Harry, you know how I get with these modern women and their divorces."

"Yes, well, Mike is a bit unorthodox for our little family business, but he's already got new business up in Mill Neck, and the dry cleaners up there have always been the toughest nuts to crack."

"Their kids are on drugs."

"How do you know this, Phyllis?"

"I can just tell. Can't you just tell?"

"I haven't looked at them real closely, but I'm sure they're good kids. Mill Neck. Those are all Bosley's. Either that son of a bitch is slipping, or Mike is that good, and I'm beginning to think the latter. We haven't had anyone like him since Bob Linderman back in the late 70s, at least until his liver gave out."

"I don't trust that playboy. I don't trust any of them. Those people have no class."

In the July heat, behind the wheel of the Rabbit heading south on the Seaford-Oyster Bay Expressway, no A/C, windows down, radio tuned to Scott Muni, commercials over, Griff reached for the volume knob and turned it up—

"Here's the new one from a band out of Seattle called Pearl Jam, this one's 'Alive', 102.7 WNEW-FM, New York," and the riff began—

"Whoa," Griff said, turning up the volume again—

At the factory office of Hillman Bros. Hanger Mfg., Co., Inc. —

"Mike, my superstar salesman, come in, come in!" said Harry, rising from his highbacked Corinthian leather executive chair.

"Howdy, Harry," Mike said, extending his hand.

"I'm breaking out the good stuff," Harry said, going over to the minibar and holding up a bottle of Johnnie Walker Blue. "I just ran the quarterly reports, and, by God, Mike, I don't know how you're doing it, but who am I to complain? I'll leave that to Phyllis." He poured the whisky into the glasses and handed one to Mike. "I never even heard of a hanger salesman working on Sundays. If this keeps up, I might get to retire a little earlier than I was planning and move down to The Villages."

"Glad to hear it, chief."

"You're not doing anything illegal, are you?" Harry smiled.

"Of course not, Harry. Just an old technique I used at Hammersmith, get 'em on a Sunday when they're relaxed. You'd be surprised how many guys are more than happy to talk business with me than spend time with their wives and children."

"Ah, the secret of your success," Harry said, raising his glass.

At Friendly's—

Griff, sans menu, looked up at D'arcy—

"Cod melt, no coleslaw, double fries, Coke, and Reese's Pieces Sunday with Butter Crunch Ice Cream."

"Whoa, what's the occasion?"

"I know where I belong."

"Phil," said Harry Hillman, looking at his aged salesman. "Your numbers for new sales have been declining for a decade. And you, Frank—Frank, are you awake over there?"

"What's that?" Frank said, shaking himself awake, hearing aid wire hanging from his ear.

"And you, Joe—"

"I'm just a little burnt out, Harry."

"You've been burnt out since 1983, Joe. Listen, guys, I don't mean to get on your case, but Mike has opened my eyes."

"Why isn't he at this meeting?"

"Because he's out there hustling for new business in the northeast quadrant, and I just wanted to tell you that, if he keeps doing what he's doing, I'm going to have no choice but to let him go into your quadrants also."

"You don't have to threaten us, Harry."

"I'm not threatening you, Phil. I'm just trying to wake you guys up. I need you guys to be like Mike."

In the office of Val Valentine, CEO of L.I. 69 Studios in Centercach—

"Cheers," Val said, raising his tumbler of Johnnie Walker Blue to Mike's. They sipped, then Val, with Gold Zippo, lit Mike's Partagás, then his own.

"I gotta hand it to you, Mike. When you told me this idea about directing a dry cleaner series and filming on site, I thought you were fucking crazy. But who knew they'd go so wild for it in Japan and Hong Kong? I *love* LaserDisc!"

"Pretty soon I should be able to secure some new shoot locations in the other quadrants."

"I don't know how you're doing it, Mike, but who am I to complain?"

Inside the Bart Mart—

"Seattle?" Bart exclaimed, puffing a Phillie. "What happened to college?"

"They have college out there. And girls. And beer. And Pearl Jam. And I'm gonna drive cross-country like Kerouac."

"Whatcha gonna do for money?"

"Find a job, I guess. They have those out there too."

"Well, if that don't cut it, I got a guy out there. They got some fine green in those parts."

"Thanks, B, for everything. You've been more of a father to me than my own father ever was."

"Alright, G. You better roll before the tears start fallin', motherfucker."

Just outside the driveway gate, Joyce watched the Rabbit pull away, the little car stuffed with everything he could squeeze into it, trash bags filled with clothes and bedsheets, milk crates containing CDs, notebooks, and novels, white electric guitar and portable amp, until she could no longer see it and no longer hear the music blasting out the open windows, then went inside.

His room had been cleaned out as if by a tenant, the blue carpet stained and worn, white spots on the light blue walls where tape had been holding up posters, blinds crookedly pulled up, mattress bare. He'd left nothing behind, a space distinctly his since he was ten now just an empty room that any kid could have grown up in, save the lingering smell of cigarettes and whatever else he'd been smoking in here.

She opened the windows and pulled down the screens, then sat on the mattress and began to cry.

Sunday afternoon, inside Bodine's Dry Cleaners in Locust Valley—

"Cut!" Mike yelled, exploding from the director's chair and approaching the frightened actors in front of one of the industrial drying machines. "Storm, are you in a hurry? Not so fast!"

"Sorry, Mike," he said, looking down at his deflating erection.

"And Lacy, come on, make it look like you're enjoying it at least a little bit!"

"Sorry, Mike," she said, sniffling.

"Alright, let's try this again, fluffer on set," he said, then, turning to his personal assistant, "Stella, pour me another drink, babe."

"Yes, Mike," she said, putting down her clipboard and scurrying to the portable bar.

The return address on the envelope bore the official State University of New York Buffalo State College seal.

She brought it to her room and, with the Waldbaum's box cutter she'd stolen from her brother's room, sliced it open and pulled out the letter.

She unfolded it and scanned down to the first paragraph, stopping at "accepted".

"Ah-ah-ah," she laughed.

In a partially occupied, twenty unit apartment building in Seattle's Capitol Hill neighborhood —

"So," said Garry Boller, landlord, in his first floor apartment, wall entirely covered with Mandala tapestries, burning incense on the coffee table, shirtless, 40s, bearded, mirrored sunglasses, long hair falling from yellow bandana, green jeans, red leather shoes, "you're, like, a banker dude or something?"

"A banker?" Griff asked.

"Yeah, man. Bankers from New York make good money, right? I'd have absolutely no problem having a banker dude sign a lease."

"Uh, yes, right. A banker. But more on the investment side. Stocks, bonds, pork bellies."

"Whoa, so you're, like, a stockbroker?"

"Uh, yeah. Kind of. Yeah. A stockbroker. On the L.I. Exchange."

"Far out, man. Stockbrokers are even better than bankers,

so, like, you're in, man. Congrats!"

He reached under the couch and retrieved a clipboard of leases photocopied so many times that not a single word of the type was legible.

"Don't worry about filling this thing out, man, just put your John Hancock down there at the bottom," he said, looking around for a pen. "And if you need any green, just let me know, I got plants growing in every closet and in a bunch of the vacant apartments."

Through the curtain she watched Mike emerge from the Trans Am and unsteadily climb the front steps.

She waited until he was inside and the door was closed.

"Hard day at the office?"

"Don't start, I'm not in the mood."

"You're never in the mood anymore."

He went to the minibar and poured himself a Johnnie Walker Red.

"Don't you think you've had enough to drink?"

"Nope," he said, then sipped.

"Mike, I think you're drinking too much."

"I don't care what you think."

"You don't care what your wife thinks?"

"Nope."

He took another sip.

"Mike—"

"Please stop talking."

"Mike—"

"I asked you nicely to please stop talking. If you say another word, I'm gonna make you stop talking."

She watched him finish the drink, then left the room when he began pouring himself another.

At the Swifty Car Rental branch in Lynnwood, Washington —

"What we do here," said Brad, Branch Manager, a morbidly obese man in an electric wheelchair behind a desk covered with Wendy's wrappers, chewing a mouthful of Big Bacon Classic Triple, sipping a 64-ounce soda, "is provide insurance replacement vehicles for people who've been in accidents and need a rental car while theirs is at the body shop being repaired. Your job will be to prep the cars and deliver them to customers at the shop, then tow them back when they're done with them. We use those pickups out there with the tow dollies and do the rental right at the shop, which is where we have the edge over those trenchcoat bastards at Enterprise with their 'We'll pick you up' bullshit, when what they're really doing is kidnapping you back to their office and hard selling you Physical Damage Waivers. Assholes. Look at them, they're out there now spying on us."

Griff turned and saw, across the shopping center in front of the Enterprise office, two guys in suits and trenchcoats looking in their direction through binoculars.

"Assholes," he said.

"Damn right. They even come in here sometimes acting all friendly, smiling, and sometimes they bring Tootsie Rolls, but it's so phony because you know they're just spying on us."

"Motherfuckers."

"Yeah."

"So, like, I would get to drive around in one of those trucks towing cars all day?"

"Yep. And prepping them. And doing the rental with the customer at the shop."

Griff looked out the window at the Dodge Rams with the Swifty logo on the doors, one with a freshly washed Antarctic Blue Chevy Corsica with front wheels strapped to the dolly.

"Awesome," he said.

In the parking lot of Hillman Bros. Hanger Mfg., Co., Inc.—

Mike, in the quiet of the Trans Am cabin, took a swig from the bottle of Johnnie Walker Black, waited, then took another, before returning it to the glove box and heading inside.

Harry was waiting for him in his office holding a bottle of Johnnie Walker Blue.

"There he is, my man!" Harry exclaimed, but his smile quickly disappeared and he put the bottle down on his desk. "Sheesh, Mike, are you alright? It looks like we need to have *you* dry cleaned."

"I'm fine, Harry."

"You're drunk, Mike."

"I'm not drunk."

"You are and I'm a little concerned."

"About what? That report in your hand? Pretty good, right?"

"Mike, these numbers are off the chart, but if this is what it's doing to you—"

"I'm fine, Harry. Just leave me be and you'll be off to The Villages in no time."

"Mike—"

"Harry, please stop talking."

"Do you need help, Mike?"

Mike took the bottle of Blue from the desk.

"Go to hell, Harry. And take that ugly old bat wife of yours with you."

At the Five Horizons Coffee House in Seattle's University District—

Jessica, owner and manager, emerged from the back and introduced herself to the applicant, Viola Inouye, then invited her to sit at one of the small round tables at the window overlooking University Way and started reading from her résumé.

"Currently at U-dub, worked at the bakery at Safeway, bakery at Asian Family Market—I take it you like to bake."

"I love baking."

"Well, if you're any good, we do sell fresh baked goods here, brownies, cookies, muffins, so you would get a chance to do some of that here."

"I make a mean butterscotch brownie."

"Butterscotch brownie? That sounds really good."

"Everyone loves it."

Joyce heard the Trans Am pull into the driveway, then a crash and the breaking of glass. She put down her burgundy and hurried to the living room window, seeing the car parked crookedly with the passenger side headlight busted where it had hit one of the marble statue pedestals.

Mike got out, leaving the door open, holding a bottle of

Johnnie Walker Blue, unlit cigarette dangling from lips, shirt untucked, several buttons undone.

"Oh my God!" she said, hurrying to the front door and opening it. "Mike, what's going on?"

"Fuck Harry Hillman," he said, then turned around and gave the finger to the Hillman house.

"Mike!"

"Come on, I know you always wanted to do that."

She waited for him to stagger inside, then closed the door and locked it.

"Mike, what happened?"

"Ungrateful loser. Hangers. Fucking loser. Fuck him and that cunt wife of his."

"Why are you so drunk?"

"Stow it, woman! I'm not drunk! God damn, if one more person says that, I'm gonna start swinging."

"You need help, Mike. You and I both know that at this point."

"You need to stop talking."

"I already called Rocky Point and asked about their alcohol rehab."

"You what?"

"I called Rocky Point and they can take you at any time."

"God damn you! I'm never going back to that fucking place!"

Breathing heavy, he looked at her, then, bottle in hand, went into the garage, slamming the door and locking it.

Hearing a noise in the yard, Stacy hit the mute button on the MTV, silencing the jagged ending of Nine Inch Nails' "Hurt".

Through the window she saw her stepfather in the yard setting up a folding ladder next to the oak tree, beneath a branch bearing the remnants of an old rope swing. On the grass beside the ladder, a coil of nautical rope with a noose at one end.

He made several attempts to throw the noose over the branch before succeeding. He then climbed the ladder and, sitting on the top cap, made some adjustments to the rope, then put the noose around his neck.

He stepped up to the top cap and the ladder wobbled wildly, but he managed to stabilize it long enough to look out at the bay, then back at the house, his eyes meeting hers.

He grinned, then the ladder wobbled again and this time fell away.

"Are you ready to begin, Mrs. Ramone?" asked Paul Marino, Mike's longtime lawyer, a balding, overweight man with metal-framed bifocals and a poorly trimmed mustache.

"Can I smoke in here?" Joyce asked.

"Of course," Paul said, pulling open a desk drawer and producing a white ashtray with the logo of the Dick Dora restaurant on its side that he placed in front of Joyce. He then pulled out a Zippo lighter and lit her cigarette.

"Thank you," she said. "Okay, I'm ready."

"Okay, here we go. To my loving wife, Joyce, the only woman who ever truly satisfied me, I leave all my worldly possessions. The end."

"That's it?"

"Yes, and he wanted me to say 'the end' like that. I'd been bugging him about writing a will, and, finally, he got fed up and told me to write down what I just read you, so we went with that."

"Okay. Well, what does that even mean? I know the house is paid for, the cars, the boat—"

"Yes, there's all that. But that's not even the good part."

"What good part?"

"The stock portfolio."

"He never mentioned it."

"I think he may have forgotten about it. He used to buy all the time, a little with each paycheck like Warren Buffett, starting in the late seventies going into the early eighties. Mostly blue chippers, and they were bargains back then, and then there's all the stock options he exercised from Hammersmith over the years without selling any of it. The value of the portfolio as of yesterday's close—twelve million, seven hundred thirty five thousand, eight hundred forty three dollars and fifty seven cents—

"..."

"Mrs. Ramone, are you okay? Mrs. Ramone, your cigarette—"

In the alley next to the Blue Moon Tavern in Seattle's U District, Griff passed the joint he'd rolled from Garry's weed to The Rastafarian.

"It is too bad your Kerouac and Cassady couldn't drive to Jamaica, they would have loved it," said The Rastafarian after taking a monster hit. "We was Beat way before him. This is good shit, mon."

"It really gives you the munchies, though."

"Have you ever been to the Five Horizons?"

"No. What is it?"

"It is a coffee shop on the University Way that sells baked goods. They make a mean butterscotch brownie, mon."

An open bottle of Four Roses bourbon atop a stack of legal papers, the top half relating to the $100 million class action lawsuit against Hillman Bros. Hanger Mfg., Co., Inc. and L.I. 69 Studios by dry cleaning establishments all over northeast Nassau County, and the bottom half relating to the bankruptcy paperwork filed shortly after Hillman Bros. lost 92% of its business when the scandal broke, 1010 WINS news radio calling it *"the biggest dry cleaning-wire hanger-pornography ring ever in the Tri-State area."*

Harry Hillman leaned back in his Corinthian leather executive chair and took a deep breath, then opened the lower desk drawer and pulled the Glock from behind the manila folders.

"The Villages," he said, then put the barrel to the side of his head and pulled the trigger.

At the Five Horizons Coffee House, just before closing —

Viola, wrapping the unsold baked goods, looked up when she heard the tinkle of the bell above the door, a guy in a Pearl Jam "Stickman" t-shirt, Old Navy cargo shorts, red beret, flannel shirt tied around waist, Timberlands without socks —

"Can I help you?" she asked.

"I hear you make a mean butterscotch brownie," he said.

In the executive conference room of Blockbuster Video headquarters in Fort Lauderdale, CEO Wayne Huizenga addressing executives from his CarTemps USA division, which had just acquired Swifty Car Rental—

"Now that the acquisition of Swifty is complete, I need you guys to focus on getting those stores converted to the CarTemps brand as swiftly as possible. We need to let those bastards at Enterprise know that we're coming after their insurance replacement business. And make sure we get all the Swifty employees drug-tested ASAP so we can get the junkies weeded out. I'm already hearing all sorts of stories about use on the job, particularly in the Northwest."

In the main lobby of the Trump Taj Mahal in Atlantic City, the final bulbs of the lighting upgrade done by Slate Bulb and Electric having just been twisted into their sockets—

"Hell of a job, Fred," said The Donald. "This is big league, baby. The one in India doesn't have lighting like this."

"Appreciate the business, Don."

"Don't ever go to India, Fred. The place smells like a sewer, and there's cow shit all over the golf courses. I would never build there. But Russia, Fred, there's a future in Russia. They just gotta get the right guy in place over there. Ever been?"

"Once. I did a job at Red Square."

"Really? Know anyone inside?"

"A couple of oligarchs."

"We're gonna have to talk more about this, but right now I've got a bunch of girls waiting for us upstairs and they're on the clock. They're expensive, Fred, but they're worth it. They're a real pisser."

In the break room at the Swifty Car Rental branch in Lynnwood—

Griff popped a dozen goldenseal capsules from the GNC blister pack and washed them down with Safeway distilled white vinegar in water cooler cone cups that would quickly spring leaks from the vinegar eating through the paper, the drips staining his white dress shirt and Jerry Garcia tie—

At LaSalle Park in Buffalo, where the unrelenting winds blowing off Lake Erie kept extinguishing the torches—

"Looks like a flashlight night," said Frank the cameraman to Reverend Virgil, referring to the flashlights covered with orange cellophane shaped like fire they used on windy nights.

"Maybe we should ask our new Lead Torchbearer," he said, looking at Stacy, now the Lead after Sister Kikimora was voted off last week. "What do you think, Sister Blednica?"

Stacy nodded.

"Then flashlights it shall be," said the Reverend, smiling.

Inside the Starr Laboratories Sample Collection Center at the Northgate Mall in Seattle—

"Griffin Ramsey," said the receptionist, looking at the computer screen. "There you are. One standard drug screening. Please fill out this form and have a seat."

"Would it be okay if I peed now? 'Cause I really gotta go."

"We don't do urine samples anymore. Now we just cut a couple of strands of your hair and send those to the lab because you can't mask drug residue in your hair. So you can use the bathroom, then come back and fill out the form."

"Oh," he said, looking out at the mall concourse, then back at the receptionist. "Actually, I'll be right back. I think I left my wallet in one of the changing rooms at JCPenney."

At the kitchen table—

"Oh," Joyce said, circling with red pen the ad in the "Personals" section of the *Newsday* classifieds:

DIVORCED WHITE MALE COP
AGE 43 STOCKY BUILD FUN
HANDSOME MAN

At Griff's, and now also Viola's, apartment on Capitol Hill—

"Check this ad out," Viola said, handing Griff *The Stranger* classifieds, the ad circled with red ink:

COME WORK FOR AN ONLINE BOOK STORE
ROCK & ROLL ATMOSPHERE
RAPID ADVANCEMENT AND STOCK OPTIONS
BRING KNEEPADS AND WINNING ATTITUDE

"What's an 'online bookstore'?" Griff asked.

"They sell books on the World Wide Web."

"The what?"

"The Information Superhighway. We have it at school now, and they gave everyone an email address."

"A what?"

"It's for electronic messages."

"…"

"Anyway, it might be a good opportunity to get in early with a tech startup like the people who got in early with Microsoft."

"I answered an ad like this when I first got out here, and, when I went to the interview, they put me in a K-Car and drove me up to the Mukilteo Speedway and dropped me off in some office park and wanted me to go door-to-door selling cookbooks. I was like, 'No way, man, this isn't a rock and roll atmosphere, assholes'," and they got mad and drove away and I had to take the bus home and transfer six times and it took like four hours."

"This isn't door-to-door. It's like mail order, except people place the order on the computer."

"Wouldn't it be easier just to call and tell them what you want or just fill out a form and drop it in the mail?"

"Not really."

"It sounds stupid. I'd rather work for a real bookstore. Barnes & Noble. Border's. B. Dalton. Waldenbooks. Wherever paperbacks are sold. Or any one of these awesome used bookstores around here."

"They sell real books, it's just the store part that's virtual. You know, like the holodeck on *Star Trek*."

"The holodeck? Really?"

"Stock options are also really good. If the company takes off, you could become a millionaire."

"What was that part about kneepads?"

"Maybe they play sports during breaks like those cool startups do. You could probably get a cheap pair from Goodwill."

At the TGI Fridays in Massapequa's Barnes & Noble shopping center—

"You know, Joyce, I never thought I'd meet a dame like you in the personals," said Sergeant Shane O'Connell, NCPD, to his date, across the red-and-white striped tablecloth. "A lot of broads see 'cop' and half of them are the same whores who hang out at the cop bars, and then the other half are degenerate males looking for a good time with a man in uniform."

"Oh, well, thank you, I think," Joyce said, sipping her Fruit Punch Margarita.

"Here, try the potato skins, they're terrific," Shane said, picking one off his plate and placing it in her basket of coconut shrimp.

In front of the open garage door of a residential home in Bellevue, Washington, books all over the floor with pieces of paper beneath them—

"I'm looking for Jeff," said Griff, standing in the drizzle, scuffed red catcher's shin guards over a pair of khaki Dockers. Inside, a dozen or so kneepadded people on the floor packing the books into boxes, including a man in his thirties with thinning hair, who stood up and started laughing maniacally.

"Hey, Johnny Bench!" he exclaimed. "Those shin guards are terrific! And so are those khakis! I'm Jeff, by the way. And you are..."

"Griff Ramsey."

"Griff Ramsey, you're hired!"

"Whoa. Really?"

"Anyone who shows up *wearing* the kneepads is automatically hired. That shows you've got a winning attitude and you're ready to step right up to the plate. Or, in your case, behind the plate. Can you start right now?"

"Uh, do you guys, like, drug test?"

"Nope!"

"Uh, okay, yeah, man, let's rock and roll! What should I do?"

"You see those books on the floor with the papers under them? Those are orders that our customers placed online. All you have to do is peel the sticker off the paper and put it on the box, then put book and paper in the box and seal it up. Simple as that."

"Is it okay if I've never been online?"

"Sure, it's easy. I'll teach you myself!"

She followed him into crowded, smoky Gannon's, the cop bar across the street from the Massapequa Park train station, mustached men with bad haircuts, scantily clad women with heavy makeup and giant hair —

"Shane, I'm actually kind of tired, I think I'd rather go home."

"We're here. We'll have a drink and say hello to my friends."

On their way to the bar he was greeted by several men who patted him on the shoulder and made crude male noises. The women glared, Joyce overhearing one say, "On what street corner did he find that old slut?"

"Shane, I really want to go home now."

"Come on, just one drink. They make a mean Rob Roy here."

In the moonlit garret bedroom of Reverend Virgil Marvin in the Black Rock neighborhood of northwest Buffalo —

She took the chalice and from it sipped their blood as he'd just done, some still in their mouths as they kissed, crimson streaking ashen chins, then she touched him —

"Oh, Blednica," he moaned.

"So, Joyce, do you mind if I come in for a cup of coffee or something?"

185

"Shane, it's been a lovely evening, but I'm really tired and need to go inside and go to sleep."

"What? That's it? A guy takes a broad out for dinner and drinks and she doesn't invite him in for a cup of coffee? Friday's ain't cheap, you know."

"I appreciate it, Shane, but—"

"You think you're too classy for me or something?"

"Shane, no, of course not. My father was a cop."

"Will you go out with me again?"

"Shane, I'm sorry, this was a lovely evening—"

"What? You're not even gonna go out with me again?"

"Good night, Shane."

She pushed open the door and stepped inside, then closed and locked it, while he continued to plead. Leaving the lights off, she went into the kitchen and waited for him to drive away, then turned on the light, sat at the table, and began to cry.

In "The Buildout", a gutted commercial office space in downtown Seattle—

"...your replacement Backstreet Boys CD is on the way, and thanks for calling *Earth's Biggest Bookstore*."

Griff hit the "AWAY" button and took off his headset, dropping it on the door desk.

"You're not supposed to say that anymore," said Chaz, his cubicle neighbor. "Jeff wants it to be, *Books, CDs, and More*."

"Fuck that, man. I came here to work for a bookstore."

In the recently purchased Trump Tower penthouse of Fred and Dolly Flynt—

Fred told Bobby Rydell and the band to stop, then took the microphone and handed it to The Donald, while the staff distributed champagne glasses filled with Don Perignon, and one with Diet Coke.

"Let's everyone give a nice hand for Fred and Dolly in their beautiful new penthouse," Donald said. "Marla and I are thrilled to have you in our building."

The guests applauded.

"You're all wonderful, this is just lovely, you should all be proud of yourselves for being here, and proud of Fred, here. He's like the guy from that book—what's that book again? Gatsby, yes, Fred is like the Great Gatsby up there on the North Shore. He built his light bulb company from scratch and look at him now, buying a penthouse in this great tower. He's big league, baby, and now Slate Bulb & Electric, the greatest bulb company ever in history, is the official light bulb company of Trump properties worldwide."

The crowd applauded again.

"And, of course, we can't forget Dolly, we all know and love her, where is Dolly? You can't miss her..."

Dolly, in gown by Ann Demeulemeester, approached the stage like a queen, smiling, waving, blowing kisses.

After the microphone was given back to Rydell, she approached Joyce with a hug.

"Thanks for coming," she said. "We don't see each other enough anymore."

"I know," Joyce said.

"And who do we have here?" asked Donald, approaching

with Marla.

"Donald, this is Joyce, my best friend since kindergarten."

"A pleasure, Joyce," he said, extending his hand.

Joyce shook his hand and Marla's.

"You were talking about Seattle before," Dolly said to Donald. "Joyce's son lives out there."

"Beautiful city," he said, "but a lot of freaks, grungy people walking around with dirty bare feet and they smell like a sewer, junkies, anarchists, militant lesbians, fish tossers, they all oughta be locked up."

In Jeff's office —

"Griff, good to see you," said the bald man, extending his hand.

"Jeff? Whoa, what happened to your hair?"

"It was going anyway, so I decided to go Telly Savalas, except without the brown cigarettes and suckers. Still got those shin guards?"

"Yeah, they're at my desk."

"We should put them in the museum." "Yeah, man, that's cool. Listen, Jeff, I gotta be honest, I don't like where this ship is headed. I just got off the phone with some woman screaming at me about not getting her Beanie Babies in time for her kid's birthday. I can't have that, man. I don't even know what the fuck a Beanie Baby is, and I'm like, 'who the fuck cares, ma'am, buy your fucking brat a book instead'—I didn't really say that, but that's what I was thinking."

"That's not very customer-centric, Griff."

"I know, man, but that's just it. If the lady called and said she didn't get her Dickens, I'd be concerned, and the customer-centricity would kick into overdrive, and someone who reads Dickens or any literature at all would probably be more polite than these losers calling with the Jerry Springer on in the background screaming at me about their Beanie Babies and Backstreet Boys and Billie Blanks."

"Your alliteration is alluring, Griff, but you're not seeing the big picture. This was never about books. It's about global domination. The Internet. Media. Politics. Space. We're gonna own it all!"

He laughed maniacally.

"Yeah, Jeff, that sounds—uh—yeah, like, to me, it was always about the books, and I don't care about that other stuff, so, I'm, like, out of here, man."

"Are you sure, Griff? You've always been rock solid on the phones and in those email queues, and you were a hell of a packer back in the day with those shin guards."

"Yeah, I'm sure, but thanks for everything, man. I hope you make a profit someday and that this thing works out for you."

In the backyard in Oceanside—

"Fire at Two Backyard Street, all units respond," said their father through the walkie-talkie, prompting Oscar Jr. and Anthony, inside the play firehouse built for them with real construction materials and running water, to spring into action, Anthony ringing the bell, Oscar Jr. connecting the hoses and turning on the water, then both hurriedly put on their boots, coats, and helmets and, nozzles in hand, ran across the yard pulling the hoses towards the controlled blaze

of a structure built with scrap wood, the Dalmatians running alongside barking encouragement—

The back door of the real house opened and their mother stuck their head out.

"Can you tell the boys lunch is ready when they're done?" she said to her husband.

"Ten-four," said Oscar Sr., watching their sons.

At Sea-Tac International Airport—

"You picked a crazy time to finally visit," said Griff, behind the wheel of Viola's Passat, to his mother in the passenger seat, as he pulled away from the terminal.

"What's going on with all these people dressed in black?" she asked, cracking the window, taking cigarettes out of Coach handbag.

"Oh, don't smoke in here, Viola doesn't like cigarette smoke."

She rolled her eyes.

"I didn't get to smoke at the airport because I was trying to get away from all those scary people. There were some on the plane and they were all over the airport here."

"It's the World Trade Organization protesters. The WTO is having a conference in town, and some people really don't like them, and the protesters are coming in from all over. I never heard of it myself until a few days ago when they started saying on the news that they were expecting protests, but that the police supposedly had it all under control."

"But why do they hate this WTO?"

"I think it has something to do with Kathie Lee Gifford using Honduran slave children to manufacture her clothing line. Here, I'll pull into this park-and-ride so we can have a cigarette."

Downtown near the Westin, where many storefront windows had been boarded with fresh Home Depot plywood already covered with graffiti, *FUCK THE WTO*, *McMeat = McMurder*, *El Barto*, anarchy symbols, Pynchon's Trystero, there were more people in black, and people dressed as sea turtles, hippies playing possum in the street, shirtless barefooted teenagers, men in drag, women with Ted Williams haircuts and unfeminine musculature, unintelligible chanting, trash receptacles on fire, police in riot gear—

"I always heard this city was nice, but it looks like a war zone," she said.

"It doesn't usually look like this."

After checking in and having her bags brought up to the suite, she got back in the car with Griff.

"So, are we going out to eat?" she asked. "I'll pay, of course."

"Actually, something better. Viola is at the apartment right now preparing a traditional Japanese meal."

"Oh. Japanese? Uh, well, I'm not eating raw fish. Or probably anything else. In fact, I was hoping to go try some fresh *cooked* seafood at a nice restaurant—"

"Probably not a good night to eat out. You don't have to eat the sushi, and, for dessert, she made her famous butterscotch brownie."

In a downtown Seattle office less than a block from the WTO conference at the Sheraton Grand—

"At least we don't seem to be in their crosshairs," said Jeff to his Number One after watching protesters smash the Planet Hollywood storefront window across the street, the chanting crowds extending up the block from the Sheraton.

"That's because most of them probably don't know we're in here, and the ones who do are our employees. A lot of people called out sick today."

"Do you think those could be the same employees leaving union propaganda in the toilet paper dispensers?"

"It's very possible. There's a big pro-union rally going on over at Memorial Stadium."

"Fire everyone who called out sick today. We'll crush those frickin' union hipsters."

He laughed maniacally.

"What about the employees still working? It's getting pretty crazy out there, and the police strongly recommended sending everyone home—"

"Make them stay."

He laughed maniacally again.

At the apartment on Capitol Hill—

Joyce pushed away her untouched bowl of miso soup.

"Do you not like it?" Viola asked.

"Not really a soup person."

Griff turned on the TV.

"Whoa," he said, leaning in towards local network affiliate KOMO's live coverage of police in riot gear hurling tear gas cannisters and shooting rubber bullets at protesters, having already driven them east out of downtown and across I-5, they were now pushing them up Capitol Hill towards Cal Anderson Park. "V, open the window!"

Griff put a tape into the VCR and started recording.

"That's our building!" he said, pointing at the TV, then running to the open window and waving his arms above his head. "They're coming towards us!"

"What?" Joyce asked.

"I see you waving!" Viola exclaimed at the TV, then joined him waving at the window, the outside crowd noise and tear gas explosions getting louder.

Joyce stared at the TV for a moment, then reached for her handbag.

"I don't care, I'm smoking in here," she said.

In the FoodTown frozen foods locker—

Lou, with motorized jack, pulled out the Ore-Ida steak cut fries, revealing a pallet of Swanson Fish & Chips TV dinners, the cases stacked crookedly with a gap in the middle and a hand sticking out.

"Holy shit!" he exclaimed, then began throwing aside boxes until uncovering a body frozen so stiff it would take three days to thaw.

"Whoa," he said. "Uncle Jimmy."

The envelope was fancy like a wedding invitation, the return address from Fred and Dolly Flynt, but it was for a thousand dollar-a-plate Western-themed fundraiser they were hosting at The Garden City Hotel for Texas Governor and Republican presidential candidate George W. Bush, with choice of prime rib or rib eye, and a handwritten note from Dolly in pink ink: *"You better be there, Joyce! Lots of rich, eligible, REPUBLICAN men will be there!"*

At the Garden City Hotel, the fundraiser a sellout, the ballroom decorated with hay bales, an old wooden wagon, red and blue rodeo barrels with big white W's—

"Rush Limbaugh is here," said one Nassau County Councilman to another, both holding plates of brisket burnt ends being served as appetizers.

"I don't think that's really Rush. Just another wannabe."

"Yeah, I think you're right. But who can blame the guy? With that look alone, he's probably getting laid all the time. What woman isn't hot and heavy for Rush?"

"All except the lesbians, I guess."

"True. Won't see any of those at this hoedown, though. Hey, check her out," he said, referring to the large, redhaired, heavily made up woman in white leather cowgirl outfit, mid-thigh length skirt, tasseled boots, tasseled jacket with blue and red chevron going around the front and back emblazoned with white stars.

"Wow, they even got a rodeo clown."

"I thought she was supposed to be a girl Evel Knievel and was gonna jump over one of those barrels on a motorbike."

"I don't wanna hear any of your oldies," said Fred Flynt, in Sheriff outfit, to Bobby Rydell, the singer and his band in Roy

Rogers outfits. "Only country and Western. Texas songs. 'Okie From Muskogee', 'Houston Oilers #1'. Shit like that. And you're ready for the square dance call?"

"We've got it, Fred," Bobby said, his eye wandering over the Sheriff's shoulder to the woman in the red Christian Dior dress.

Fred turned and saw Joyce standing near a man who looked like Rush Limbaugh.

"Good," Fred said, still looking at her.

Seeing Fred and Bobby Rydell looking in her direction, Joyce turned to the portly, balding man next to her in the dark blue suit smoking a cigar.

"Excuse me," she said. "Are you here alone?"

"Why, yes, ma'am, I am traveling stag tonight and am proud to do so."

"Would you like to be my date?"

"Really?"

"Yeah?"

"You're not, like, making fun of me, are you?"

"No. Totally serious. Trust me, I'll be right by your side the whole time."

"Well, then, I'd be honored. Barry O'Doul's the name."

"Joyce Ramone," she said, shaking his hand, then kissing his cheek.

In northwest Buffalo—

"It is time," said the Reverend Virgil to Sister Blednica.

She nodded, then took from him the warm chalice filled with a concoction of black tea, mescaline, each other's blood, and other bodily fluids.

"Drink, my love," he said.

They passed the chalice until it was drained, then made love, then vomited, both remaining nude on the bathroom floor huddled and shivering until they heard a man calling from downstairs in a friendly voice, "Hello? Anyone home? Hell-oo-ooo—"

The lovers looked at each other, then got up and, still nude and holding hands, walked on down the hall to the top of the stairs, stopping when they saw the bearded, longhaired man in robes and sandals and crown of thorns down at the bottom.

"Jesus," uttered the Reverend Virgil Marvin, breathing heavy, Blednica clutching him tighter.

In a Honeymoon Suite atop the MGM Grand in Las Vegas, nude, in bed, after making love as man and wife for the first time, wed earlier in the day by an Elvis impersonator in a drive-thru chapel, then later seeing Pearl Jam downstairs at the arena—

"I can't believe they played 'Crown of Thorns'," Griff said. "I was like, 'whoa'."

"This day couldn't have been any better," Viola said, then kissed Griff. "And now I can't wait to get out to L.A."

"Oh, yeah, about that, babe, I had to like, call the broker back in Des Plaines when my ATM card didn't work, and that's when he told me the news, that, like, my stock account was tapped, and so was my checking account, and my savings, in fact, I was a bit overdrawn and the credit cards are maxed out—"

"What? I thought you had enough to pay for this trip *and* my NYU Law!"

"Yeah, like, so did I, but then the bubbles burst and now the stock is worth a lot less, and this trip has been way more expensive than I anticipated, like, *way* more expensive."

"Griff! What are we gonna do? We can't even go back to Seattle, we let the lease run out!"

"I know. Garry's already using our apartment as another grow room."

"We'll be homeless when we check out tomorrow!"

"Sorry, babe. Maybe you should take over the finances going forward."

"What finances? We're broke and neither of us have jobs! I won't even be able to make my student loan payment! I'll have to defer!"

"Bummer, babe. Alright, here's what we'll do. I'll call my mother, and she can send us a couple of plane tickets to New York, First Class, and then we can crash at her place for a while, and get her to pay for your law school—"

"She would do that? I always get the feeling that she doesn't like me."

"She probably doesn't, but don't sweat it. I love your parents, by the way. But, yeah, I think I can get her to pay. She's, like, a million-heiress."

At Buffalo's Broderick Park, on the shore of the Niagara River—

"I'll just stay right here," said Jesus, standing on the river's surface. "I'm a warm water guy, so, Buffalo in October, no thanks. You guys just dunk each other, and I'll officiate."

Both nude, Virgil carried Stacy into the 55 degree water and dunked her backwards, then lifted her out.

"Whoa!" Jesus said, clapping. "You're in, Stace! Congrats and amen! I'd be screaming my ass off in that water, but you didn't flinch! Bye-bye, Beelzebub! Alright, Virge, your turn!"

In Biltmore Shores, Election Night 2000, polls about to close in the first seven states—

"Who is it?" Barry called from the den to Joyce at the front window.

"Oh, God, it's Griff and his girlfriend, and they have luggage."

She stepped outside as they were coming up the platform steps.

"You should have called," she said to Griff.

"Why? Do you have a man in there?"

"Yes. His name is Barry and he lives here now and we're getting married next year."

"Whoa. Far out."

"And, just so you know, he's very passionate about politics, so please don't say anything that'll scare him away. Hello, Viola."

"Hi, Mrs. Ramone. Nice to see you."

"What are you doing here anyway? I thought you hated Long Island."

"Viola wants to go to NYU Law. Oh, by the way, we just got married in Vegas."

"What?"

"Yeah, by an Elvis impersonator."

"Oh. Well, congratulations, I guess, and come on in."

Barry emerged from the den.

"Hello, Griff, nice to meet you," he said, extending his hand.

"Whoa, you're that fat idiot from the radio," Griff said, not accepting the handshake. "Ma, you didn't tell me you were marrying this bloated turd!"

"He's not Rush Limbaugh," Joyce said.

"Even if he's not—Jeez—and you used to be married to The Hammer—"

"Griff!"

"Your mother tells me you're a liberal," Barry said.

"Nah, man, I listen to Howard. Baba Booey!"

In Studio C of Community Access Channel 79 Studios, Buffalo—

"Well, this is different," said Frank the cameraman, taking in the Reverend Virgil Marvin's white silk suit and clean shaven face, save the fine pencil mustache, hair still slicked back.

"We're changing the format."

"Uh-oh. Did you jump the shark?"

"Did I what?"

"Format changes usually signal the beginning of the end."

"Yes, well, I have found a path out of the darkness for our followers, so we'll be doing the show from in here going forward."

"They're not going to allow torches in here."

"There will be no Torchbearers."

"No Torchbearers? Whoa."

"I want the studio to be bright and gay, blue skies and heavenly clouds and rainbows and gold crosses on the greenscreen, Beckett chairs and plinth coffee table from Ethan Allen, Stacy seated next to me—"

"Who's Stacy?"

"My wife, the former Sister Blednica."

In Griff's old bedroom, now a guest room—

"I don't think I can stay here any longer," Viola said, she and Griff nude under the covers.

"We've only been here three days, babe."

"Have you asked your mother about paying for my law school?"

"Yeah. She said no."

"Did she say why?"

"She said something about the money being tied up in mutual funds, but I could tell she was lying. I think you're right about her not liking you."

"Ugh. Now what are we gonna do?"

"No worries, babe. Tomorrow I'm gonna cross the border and see a guy I used to work for. He runs a lot of local businesses. I'm sure he'll have something for me."

"Cross the border? What border?"

"The county border. But don't worry, I'll be fine. He's an old friend, kind of like a father to me. He'll help us get out of here."

In Studio C—

"Well, Stacy," said the Reverend Virgil Marvin, viewers at home seeing gold crosses floating across the heavenly azure behind them, "it's been a wonderful first show in the light, and we would like to thank everyone for tuning in. God Bless you all, in the name of Jesus Christ, amen."

The "ON AIR" light went dark and Virgil and Stacy started removing their microphones.

"Wow, that was—very, very different," Frank said, stepping out from behind the camera. "Are you sure your followers are going to buy in? I mean, haven't people been trying to push Jesus on them their whole lives, and they turn to you to get away from that?"

"Coming from me," said the Reverend Virgil Marvin, "it will be different."

At the Bart Mart—

"You just here to say hello, or you here for somethin' else?" Bart asked, behind the glass, puffing a Phillie.

"V wants to go to NYU Law and the Million-heiress won't pay for it."

"So, you tellin' me you want back in the game, and you need to go big."

"Yeah. And no freezers or milk crates, please."

"Alright, G. I actually got something right up yo alley."

In northwest Buffalo—

Led by Sister Kikimora, the procession of cowled former Torchbearers, carrying unlit tiki torches and red gasoline cans, surrounded the home of the Reverend Virgil Marvin and the former Sister Blednica and doused the exterior, then, at Kikimora's whistle, lit their torches and ignited the old wooden structure with a wall of flame that left little chance of escape for anyone sleeping inside, then extinguished their tikis and left the property, scattering unseen into the Buffalo night.

At Royal Lanes bowling alley, West Hempstead—

"Yo, I need a pair of size thirty shoes," said the dude in the Jay-Z shirt in front of the counter.

On the other side, Griff pulled from one of the cubbies a pair of weathered size 11 Brunswicks and placed one on the counter, into which the dude slipped some bills. Griff took it back and put the other shoe on the counter, from which the dude palmed a rolled plastic sandwich bag containing an eighth of BC Neko Kush Cake, then disappeared into the Long Island night.

In the studio of Rush Limbaugh—

"Next we have Barry from Massapequa," said the host, puffing a Macanudo.

"Hey, Rush. We should ban immigration outright. Just say, 'That's it, we're full.' Maybe we'll start letting them in again after we flush out the ones from the bad countries, and there's plenty of those."

"There sure are, Barry," Rush said, puffing. "Next we have Ira from Staten Island calling from Jets' practice."

In the offices of Eli Jones Investments on the 87th floor of the World Trade Center South Tower, president and CEO Eli Jones on the phone with his wife, Kathy—

"You're not going to believe this," he said, "but a plane just hit the North Tower."

"What? You mean, like, one of those little planes?"

"No, a big one. An airliner. There's a huge fire."

"Oh my God."

"Yeah. I can't even imagine how many people must be dead."

"Should you get out of there?"

"It just happened a minute ago. No one's told us to leave or anything."

"Maybe you should."

"Yeah, maybe. Alright, let me see what's going on, and I'll call you back in a bit."

"Okay. I love you."

"I love you too."

Oscar jumped off the truck and looked up, the top of the tower no longer visible above the flames and smoke, the sky no longer blue.

Making their way through the lobby, he and Walsh heard the crash outside of something landing on and crushing the roof of a parked Port Authority Police cruiser, followed by screams outside and in.

"What the hell was that?"

"I think they're jumping from the top."

"Jesus."

There was another odd sound outside and a spray of red on one of the windows, followed by more screams.

They stopped at the staircase door, out of which flowed a seemingly endless stream of humanity.

"Ready to head up?" Walsh asked. "I know I could use the exercise."

"Yeah, let's go," Oscar said. "I've always meant to get up there."

At the Bart Mart—

"I'm thinking about retiring," Bart said, behind the glass, puffing a Phillie.

"Retiring? I thought you said you'd never retire."

"I know, G. But I've owned this place almost thirty years and now I keep feeling that there's gotta be more to life than sitting behind this glass counting my stacks. Maybe I'd be happier sitting on a beach in Jamaica smoking a fattie watching the ladies go by in their bikinis."

"You should do it, B."

"I'm seriously thinking about it, G."

Rush, in his studio, puffing an Opus X—

"Next we have Barry from Massapequa," he said.

"Rush, this is a no-brainer. I mean, how can we not bomb Iraq? Saddam has already invaded us by putting West Nile Virus in our mosquitoes, and now we know he's got a huge cache of chemical weapons buried all over the desert over there that could ultimately be used on us."

"Salient points, Barry," Rush said, puffing. "Next on the line, Mike from Mahopac."

At the Nassau Veterans Memorial Coliseum, where Pearl Jam, touring in support of their latest LP, *Riot Act*, had just finished the encore with "Alive", the sellout crowd screaming for more—

In the third row, Griff and Viola, surrounded by people in FDNY and NYPD merch, cheered with everyone else when the band came back out, Eddie now wearing a shiny silver sport coat and a rubber mask depicting President George W. Bush, Stone strumming the chords to "Bu$hleaguer", Matt behind his kit keeping the beat, while, on the other side of the stage, Jeff and Mike exchanged uncertain glances as Eddie hung the Bush mask on a microphone stand and began feeding it wine and kissing it, quieting the cheers to a

confused murmur—

"Bush sucks!" Griff yelled, prompting a grin from Ed, while the other people in their row began chanting "U-S-A!"

"Bush sucks!" Griff yelled even louder, just as he and Viola started getting pelted with quarters being thrown from behind.

"Griff, stop!" Viola pleaded, clutching his arm.

"Bush sucks!" he continued, until a large, bald man in front of them wearing an NYPD t-shirt turned around and punched him in the nose, and down he went.

"Fuck the police!" he yelled from the Coliseum floor, nose bleeding. "9-1-1's a joke!"

Audience members in the second, third, and fourth rows pounced, kicking and punching him until Coliseum security managed to pull him from the row and escort he and Viola out of the arena while the crowd continued to vent their rage at the silver surfer up on stage.

Out on the concourse, a pair of EMS workers attended to Griff.

"We're gonna get you to a hospital," one of them said. "At best, you only have a broken nose, a couple of cracked ribs, and a bump on the head, but they're gonna make sure you don't have any internal bleeding or head injuries."

In the downstairs bathroom—

Barry positioned the hamper in front of the toilet and placed on it the open laptop, then removed his pants and underwear and took a seat on the bowl.

He opened his browser and navigated to PornWorld and had just logged in when the chest pains began—

"Oh, crap, no," he said, then there was a sharper pain, and his body began trembling.

Clutching his chest with his numb left hand, he spent the next minute with his right hand on the scratched scroll pad attempting to get the cursor in the right spot to X out the PornWorld window before he was finally able to close it. He then reached for his trousers and pulled his flip phone from the front pocket and, on the fifth attempt, managed to hit the correct digits—

"9-1-1, what's your emergency?"

"I'm having a—ugh—heart attack—"

"Barry, is that you?"

"Yes, oh, hi Martha, looks like I'm having—ugh—another one "

"Okay, Barry, just sit tight and I'll dispatch an ambulance—"

Behind a triage curtain in the Emergency Room at Nassau County Medical Center—

"Fortunately, there doesn't seem to be any internal bleeding," said Dr. Michaels to Griff, "but you do have a concussion, so we're going to keep you overnight for observation. Just take it easy on the morphine button."

Minutes later, the doctor gone—

"I'm still alive," Griff moaned to Viola.

"You'd better be," she said, running a finger through his hair, "because I'm pregnant."

"Whoa…"

Inside the Sunrise XXX Adult Superstore on Sunrise Highway in East Islip, Suffolk County —

Joyce, in black wig and Nina Ricci sunglasses, left the lingerie section and went to the sex toys, where her eyes landed on the smiling mug of her late second husband —

"Oh my God," she said, removing the package from the hook, a dildo called "The Hammer" made by L.I. 69 Studios *"Cast from the mold of the late actor's maximum erection!"*, the back of the package including a screengrab of Mike about to enter a woman with an expression of fearful excitement.

"Good choice," said the woman behind the counter. "Me and all my girlfriends have *The Hammer* and we love it. Will that be cash or charge, ma'am?"

"Cash," Joyce said, removing from her handbag a Citibank envelope filled with crisp twenties.

In a 5,000 square foot townhouse in Manhattan's West Village —

Viola, six months pregnant with twin boys, asked the Warburg Realty agent if she could give them a minute.

"Of course," the agent said, then left the room.

"Well, V?" Griff asked.

"Can we really afford it?"

"Yeah, and then some. I have a pallet full of cash in a storage locker across the border."

"Then I love it!"

In the waiting room of the nondenominational maternity ward at Long Island Jewish—

Dr. and Dr. Inouye, after meeting their son in-law's mother and husband, chose seats on the other side of the room.

After a minute, whispering in Japanese—

"This room is too small," Dr. Inouye said to her husband.

"I agree. Should we go down to the cafeteria and get some coffee?"

"They might follow us."

From across the room, with a look on her face, Mrs. O'Doul said, "Looks like rain. Does it rain a lot in San Francisco?"

"Not enough," Dr. Inouye answered.

"We have something of a rainy season," added Dr. Inouye, "but the West, in general, has been in a prolonged drought, much in part due to climate change."

Mr. O'Doul, unwrapping a package of Twix, looked up.

"There's a lot of talk about climate change," he said, "but none of it's proven."

The Inouyes exchanged glances.

"Mr. O'Doul, there is a mountain of scientific data, studies, white papers, satellite images, effects that can be seen with the naked eye—"

"Well, *Doctor*, these scientists have convenient ways of manipulating data to suit their own agendas."

"This is a serious charge, Mr. O'Doul. Do you know of any examples of such manipulation?"

"Well, I can't think of any off the top of my head, but you can look it up on the Web. There's plenty of examples, but be sure to check the bottom of the search results, that's where Google tries to bury the truth. There's also been a lot about it on TV."

"On what network?"

"Fox News."

The Inouyes again exchanged glances.

"Don't respond," whispered Dr. Inouye to her husband.

In the birthing suite—

"Griff, lean in a little more," directed Nurse Joan, holding the digital camera, Viola on the bed with a twin in each arm. "Okay, perfect!"

She snapped the picture, then took another.

"Our first family photo," Griff said, smiling at Eijiro Ōe, then at Ichiro Ti Jean Kerouac, both boys looking back at their father in marble-eyed wonder.

"Aww, they love their daddy," said Nurse Joan. "Want to see the picture?"

"Aww," said Griff and Viola, looking at the display screen, then at their sons.

Election night 2008, in the TV den, Massapequa—

"I'm calm, really, I am," Barry said, looking at The Facebook.

"You're red as a lobster and typing really loud," Joyce said.

"Sorry, hon. Crazy night. Something's not right. Ohio? Florida? *Iowa?* How are these states going for a black man named 'Obama' over McCain? The guy's a war hero, for Chrissake. An *American* war hero. Is Obama even American? Ugh—"

He fell over in his chair, clutching his chest, trembling.

Joyce rolled her eyes.

"Alright, away from the computer," she said, pointing the remote and turning off the TV. "Go lie down on the couch, legs raised, and I'll call 9-1-1."

In the downstairs TV den of the West Village townhouse—

"Noo-Noo!" Eijiro exclaimed.

"Noo-Noo!" Ichiro repeated.

"Whoa, a sentient vacuum cleaner," Griff said.

"Tinky Winky!" Eijiro exclaimed.

"Tinky Winky!" Ichiro repeated.

"Whoa, a transgender Teletubby," Griff said.

Inside the studio classroom at the Jean-Claude Kenney Drawing Academy in Sunrise Mall, adult beginner's nude drawing class—

The strapping, early twenty-something male model dropped his robe, then took a pose on the stool and the students put pencils to easeled pads, including Joyce, drawing lefthanded.

"Such acute realism!" exclaimed Monsieur Jean-Claude over Joyce's shoulder, startling her. "It is rough around the edges, yet I have never seen such detail in a beginner's drawing class! It is like you were born with a special ability that has gone completely undeveloped. What did you say your name was again?"

"JoAnne," she said, the rest of the class leaving their easels to gather around hers, as well as the model, who put his robe on and came over.

"And you say you have never drawn before, Ms. JoAnne?"

"Uh, not really, not since eighth grade art class."

"I know a gallery owner in Manhattan who would love this—"

"No! In fact, I actually have to get going, I forgot I had a hair appointment—here's your pencil back."

She tore the drawing from the pad and hastily folded it, then stuffed it into her handbag and hurried out of the studio.

"Ms. JoAnne, will you be coming back next week?" Monsieur Jean-Claude called after her, but received no reply.

Inside the National Hurricane Center in Miami-Dade County, where Rico had just returned to his cubicle with a fresh cup of Havana blend from the K-Cup machine—

"Mother of God!" Sonny exclaimed in the cubicle next door, stubbing out his Marlboro.

"You alright over there, partner?"

"It's Sandy. She's re-forming. It looks really bad."

"Nah. They always look like they're starting to re-form after they pass through Cuba from the south, then they shrivel like a New York virgin."

"The water's warmer than usual."

"You worry too much."

"Tell me about it, partner," he said, removing a hard pack

of Marlboros from the pocket of his white linen sport coat, leaning back, putting his sockless, boat-shoed feet on the desk. "Looks like I picked the wrong day to quit the cowboy killers."

In Limbaugh's studio—

"Barry in Massapequa," Rush said, puffing a Don Carlos.

"I'm so sick of this left-wing climate change hysteria, Rush. Are we, as Americans, really going to let every little storm send us fleeing from our homes like a Clinton? Well, not I, sir. Call me when there's a real emergency."

"Well said, as usual, Barry. God bless, you're a true patriot. Next on the line, Rusty from Kansas."

On the roof in Biltmore Shores, Joyce and Barry tied to the chimney with nautical rope, the rest of the house having been engulfed by the Great South Bay as Superstorm Sandy raged—

"You see, this isn't so bad!" Barry shouted over the 70 MPH wind.

"Idiot!" Joyce shouted back. "We should have evacuated like they told us to!"

"The government can't mandate us to leave our private property, which it is our Constitutional right to defend against any and all threats, including left wing climate change hysteria—"

"Shut up!"

"Well, what did you want us to do? Cower in the wake of

these lefty libtard alarmists with their unproven global warming nonsense?"

"Shut up!"

"Honey, this is no big deal. When it's over, I'll call Servpro and they'll make it good as new—"

"If you say one more word, I'm gonna untie your rope!"

"But, honey—"

"I mean it, Barry, one more word!" she shouted, hands on his knot.

Griff stopped typing when he heard Viola call from downstairs.

"Just a second," he called back, finishing the sentence, then rolling out of his Ethan Allen Corinthian leather writing chair and going downstairs, halting when he saw Viola standing behind identical twin girls.

"What's going on?" he asked.

"Hi, Daddy," Eijiro said.

"We want to be she/her/hers now," said Ichiro.

"You want to be what now?"

"They're changing their pronouns," Viola said.

"Oh. What's a pronoun again?"

"He/him/his. She/her/hers. They/them/theirs."

"Huh?"

"They are going to identify as girls from now on."

"Whoa. Wow. This is heavy." He looked at the girls. "But hey, that's cool. I'm proud of you. What you just did is really hard. You should be who you are. That's the only way you'll ever be happy."

He took a knee and opened his long arms, and they

allowed themselves to be enveloped like they did when they were little.

"I love you guys," he said. "Girls, I mean—"

"We love you too, Daddy," they said, Griff motioning Viola to join the hug.

In a VIP suite at the Hotel National, Moscow, now illumined by bulbs purchased from Slate Bulb and Electric—

Fred Flynt, in a crimson silk robe with the hotel's gold crest on the breast pocket, pointed his tumbler of Scotch at one of the four naked women, this one skinny with dark, curly hair and smaller breasts than the others.

"What's your name, doll?"

"Yustina."

"Yustina, sweetheart, ever hear of a Cleveland steamer?"

Easter Sunday, in the newly reconstructed O'Doul house jacked up on marble stilts, their chimney now the highest point in Biltmore Shores—

Joyce opened the door and saw, standing in front of Griff and Viola, two blond-haired, blue-eyed Asian girls in yellow dresses and bonnets.

"Kon'nichiwa o bāchan!" they said together.

"What the?" Joyce said, pushing open the storm door. "Griff, where are the boys? And who are these girls?"

"Hi, mom, Happy Easter! These are the twins, except they changed their pronouns to 'she/hers'."

"They changed their what?"

"They also changed their names. Eijiro is now 'Chouko', which, in Japanese, means 'butterfly child', and Ichiro is now 'Kamiko', which means 'little goddess'."

"Is this a joke? Are you trying to ruin my Easter?"

"We just want to be ourselves, Grandma," said Chouko.

"Haven't you always wanted to be yourself, Grandma?" Kamiko asked.

In the Trump Tower boardroom —

"When I win," Donald said to Fred, "I'm going to need you to be my Secretary of Energy. You in?"

"Whatever you need, Don."

"To be honest, Fred, I didn't even know this would be someone I would have to pick, but, as soon as they told me, I said, 'I know the guy, his name is Fred Flynt, he's a good man, a decent man, a loyal man, a man who bought one of my beautiful penthouses, a Republican man, a true American, unlike that fraud Obama or that nasty Hillary, and Fred's one of the good Republicans, not one of the pussy Republicans, no, Fred Flynt's no pussy, he gets a lot of pussy, but he's no pussy, and he's the greatest light bulb guy ever, big league, even better than Edison, and he gets more pussy than Edison ever did' —"

In the kitchen, the invitation to the Flynt election night party at their Trump Tower penthouse on the counter —

"I really, really, *really* don't want to go," Joyce said to Barry.

"This is a once in a lifetime opportunity, hon! I mean, just imagine he wins, and he stops by the party, and we'll be there—"

"He's not going to win and he's not going to stop by the party."

"He's been there before."

"Yes, but not on nights he's running for president. He probably won't even be in the building."

"Why don't you want to go? I thought Dolly was your best friend."

"She is. But I've never liked Fred, and their parties are always too wild."

"Please, honey… pleeeeeease…"

His eyes were welling, a tear breaking free and streaking down his cheek.

Joyce rolled her eyes and reached for her cigarettes.

Barry sniffled.

"Fine, we'll stop by, but we're not staying long," she said, lighting and exhaling.

Election night 2016, inside the Flynt penthouse, muted flatscreens tuned to Fox News, Bobby Rydell and his band performing surprisingly raucous covers of "Rockin' in the Free World" and "Fuckin' Up", retired Islander and Met players getting chippy, chants of "Lock her up!" every time Hillary's scowling face appeared on the screens and "Forty-five!" whenever they showed Trump's smiling mug—

During Bobby and the band's rendition of "Enter

Sandman", someone yelled to stop the music and turn up the TVs.

"Holy shit, Trump's gonna win!" someone exclaimed.

The room burst into wild cheers when the graphic appeared declaring Donald J. Trump the 45th President of the United States.

"This is unbelievable!" Barry exclaimed, kissing Joyce.

"Amazing," she said. "I'm just gonna use the bathroom, then we're going."

He made a face, but she ignored it and went down the hallway into one of the powder rooms.

When she was done and opened the door, Fred was standing there. No one else was in the hallway.

"Oh, hi, Fred, you startled me."

"Hi, sweetheart," he said, phlegmy. "Quite a night."

"Oh, I know, amazing—"

"Come with me."

"What?"

He put his hand on the small of her back and forcefully escorted her down the hall, away from the party. She tried to resist, but he was too strong.

"Fred, what are you doing?"

"Stop talking."

He pushed her into a guest suite and followed her in, locking the door.

"Fred, please, what is this?"

"I've been waiting a long time for this, sweetheart."

"Fred, no—"

"You're the one I wanted. But I was stupid and let that moron Roger have him."

"You guys were friends!"

"Guys like me don't have friends."

"Fred, no—"

"Take your clothes off or I'm gonna tear them off."

"Fred, please—"

"Just do as I say and you won't get hurt, sweetheart," he said, unbuckling his belt. "You might even like it."

Heading north on BC-21 in the Kootenay region of British Columbia, Canada, traveling in a replica Metallic Pea Road Queen Family Truckster with a fake Aunt Edna tied to the roof—

"Here we are, kids, up and at 'em!" exclaimed Griff, behind the wheel, pulling into Alex's North of the Border Gifts & Gas. "Look, they even have Marty Moose in a Mountie uniform out front. Praise Mountie Moose, ha-yuck!"

"I want to go home!" Kamiko cried from the back seat.

"Me too!" cried Chouko, next to her.

"We've already talked about this," said Viola, in the passenger seat.

"I don't want to live on a farm!"

"Me neither! I want to go back to New York City!"

Griff cut the ignition and pulled the key, but the car continued to knock and shake.

"Do you want to know what I think?" he asked, wide-eyed, looking at each. "I think we should get a picture of me pretending to punch the moose in the nose, then we'll just chill out up here on the farm until about 2020, then we'll see what happens."

On a ten acre compound in Centereach belonging to the Strong Island Boys militia, dozens of vehicles parked in a field behind the main building, Hummers, Jeeps, Harley Davidsons, vintage Chevy Corsicas, pickup trucks with extra-wide sideview mirrors, Sarah Palin pinup air fresheners hung from rearviews, propane grills and meat smokers wafting clouds into the Suffolk night, a band playing Lynyrd Skynyrd and Kid Rock covers, wolves howling in the pine barrens—

Barry gravitated towards the newcomers, some watching the band, some talking, all drinking beer and eating red meat without utensils.

"So, where ya from, Barry?" asked Rick from Ronkonkoma.

"Massapequa."

"Massapequa? Wait, are you Barry from Massapequa?"

"That's me."

"Holy shit! Guys, it's Barry from Massapequa!"

In the White House Rose Garden, where, despite the raging COVID-19 pandemic, over 150 mostly maskless guests had assembled for a ceremony honoring United States Supreme Court nominee Amy Coney Barrett—

"Look at that pussy over there wearing a mask," said President Donald Trump to Secretary of Energy Fred Flynt and Counselor to the President Kellyanne Conway. "He's probably buddies with that little peckerhead Fauci."

"So, Fred, what are you doing after the ceremony?" asked

Counselor Conway, inching closer.

"Don and I have some business to attend to."

"Can I come?"

"No," said President Trump.

"Too bad 'Big Wendy' had to be here."

"Only we're supposed to use that code name, Counselor Conway," said Secret Service Agent Sullivan, who'd already several times given her the same admonishment.

In the lobby of the Moon Palace Resort, Ocho Rios, Jamaica—

"Are you sure you wish to check out so soon, Mr. Bart?" asked the woman behind the front desk. "There are still four nights left on this nonrefundable reservation. If there was a problem with the room, we can change you to another."

"Nah, everything was cool," Bart said, removing the unlit Phillie from his lips. "This place is beautiful, and everyone's been real nice, and the food is good, and there's lots of pretty ladies, but this life ain't for me. Everyone back home says my place is a dump and that I should go somewhere else, but, whenever I do, I'm counting down until it's time to go back. So, hell, maybe it is a dump, but it's my dump. It's the only place I ever feel comfortable, know what I'm sayin'?"

"I do know what you are saying," she smiled. "You are talking about your home."

"Yeah," he said, nodding. "Home."

In the "COVID Wing" at MedStar Georgetown University Hospital, Washington DC, just outside the room where Secretary of Energy Fred Flynt and his wife Delores lie unconscious, tubes down their throats, hooked up to GMC Professional Grade ventilators—

Dr. Morris Stanley looked both ways, then opened the door and stuck his head in.

"Fucking morons!" he shouted through his face shield, then snapped a photo of them on his iPhone and moved on.

At the Freedom Plaza Ellipse, Washington DC, January 6, 2021, a chilly, gray morning but red, white, and blue everywhere, as well as orange, white, and blue on the Confederate flags, and yellow and black on the Don't Tread on Me flags, and a blond girl in pigtails selling little Betsy Ross flags for ten dollars apiece, bloody Jesuses on Crucifixes, scarecrows depicting top Democrats and Vice President Mike Pence hung from gallows, men draped in animal skins, women dressed as Xena: Warrior Princess, and, up onstage, Roger Stone, Rudy Giuliani, Alex Jones, and President Trump delivering a fiery speech—

—we're going to try and give our Republicans, the weak ones because the strong ones don't need any of our help, we're going to try and give them the kind of pride and boldness that they need to take back our country. So let's walk down Pennsylvania Avenue—

The Strong Island Boys marched with their fellow patriots to the Capitol, storming the building and finding their way to Nancy Pelosi's office, taking pictures with their phones of each other posing in her chair with an unlit cigar, including Barry, who, during his turn, felt the familiar stabbing pain and clutched his chest, the others thinking he was horsing around and taking pictures until he slumped over —

"Barry!" shouted Rick from Ronkonkoma, shaking him in the chair, knocking over several framed photographs. "Come on, Barry, we gotta get out of here!"

"He don't look too good," said Larry from Lindenhurst.

"Barry! Barry!"

"We gotta get him out of here!"

They tried to lift him, but his girth and weight proved too much for the overweight, post middle-aged white men to maneuver out of the tight space behind her desk, and, after ten or so seconds of struggle, they let his body fall back in the chair, breaking one of the casters and sending a coffee cup full of pens and Sharpies to the floor.

"We have to leave him," Rick said, out of breath, hands on knees.

"Yeah," Larry agreed, and the Strong Island Boys left their brother-patriot behind, head lolled, mouth open, tongue hanging out, unlit cigar on chest, an image that would, within seconds, go viral as patriots and media streaming through the office snapped thousands of photos of the man the world would henceforth know as "The Dead Guy in Nancy Pelosi's Chair".

At the Ramsey Cannabis Farm in the Kootenays, British Columbia—

Out in the fields, wearing tan corduroy overalls with embroidered Grateful Dead bears dancing across the front pocket containing his roach tin, Griff took one last hit from his "Triple-Marley", then stubbed it out on the bottom of his boot and dropped it in the tin.

With his favorite, red-handled bud clippers, he snipped for a few more minutes, then said, "Break time," and headed towards the house.

Approaching the back kitchen door, he was greeted by the aroma of freshly baked butterscotch brownie.

In the kitchen sat the full tray cooling on the stove top, unattended.

"Whoa," he said, then looked around and listened for a moment before quietly pulling a butter knife from the drawer.

He cut a small piece from the corner and ate it. Then he cut a slightly larger piece, and a larger one after that, eventually abandoning knife and tearing off chunks with his hands—

"Griff!" Viola yelled.

"Sorry," Griff said, mouth full, crumbs on fingertips. "These things are, like, too good. My sugar addiction totally kicked in."

"Griff, that was the batch with the Golden Goose!"

"The what?"

"The stuff with the 57% THC!"

"Oh, mama, is it getting warm in here?"

"Griff, are you okay? Your eyes are glazing!"

"My heart is—ugh—beating at light speed!"

"Oh my God, you're turning purple!"

He grunted and clutched his chest, then staggered around the kitchen, bouncing off the refrigerator and knocking the K-cup machine off the counter.

"It's the big one, V!" he exclaimed, one hand on heart and the other in the air, then made a sound like a donkey that had just been shot in its hindquarters and dropped to the floor.

March 2031, at the Rocky Point Meadows Assisted Living Facility, outside the room of patient Joyce O'Doul, who'd just been found slumped in front of her easel with a nearly finished oil painting of a nude man leaning against a yellow Mustang parked in front of the Chelsea Hotel —

"So sad," Zayden said, sneaking a quick-hit from her vape pen and passing it to her colleague, Katniss.

"She was, like, such a good painter," Katniss said.

"She was married to a famous porn star. Ever hear of The Hammer?"

"Who hasn't? He's only, like, the greatest porn star of all time."

"I think she was also married to that guy who, like, stormed the government and died in that lady's chair."

She took out her phone and Googled "the guy who stormed the government and died in the lady's chair" and found hundreds of images and memes of the fat dead guy with his tongue hanging out.

"Eww, gross," Katniss said, looking away.

Made in the USA
Middletown, DE
23 October 2023

41112440R00137